Elaine Proctor made numerous political documentaries in her native South Africa before graduating from the National Film and Television School with her first feature film *On The Wire* (British Film Institute award for best first film). She then wrote and directed the feature films *Friends* (official selection of the Cannes film festival) and *Kin*, both distributed globally to critical acclaim. She wrote the film script *Paradise and the Dog of Plenty* and the BBC television thrillers *Loaded* and *City of Gold*. *Rhumba* is her first novel.

# RHUMBA

Elaine Proctor

Quercus

First published in 2011 by

Quercus
55 Baker Street
7th Floor, South Block
London
W1U 8EW

A CIP catalogue record for this book is available
from the British Library

ISBN 978 0 85738 508 6

10 9 8 7 6 5 4 3 2 1

Typeset by Ellipsis Digital Limited, Glasgow

Printed and bound in Great Britain by Clays Ltd, St Ives plc

For Lucia and Jacob, who are my everything.

For my mother Lynda Proctor
who will never be able to read this book
but who made it necessary for me to write it.

For all the people in Tottenham and beyond
who told me their stories and showed me their worlds.

And for David.

*Part One*

# The Roof

Flambeau hunted birds on the rooftop all that early summer's day.

He took the stairs two at a time and ran through the red metal door with his catapult in his pocket. The boy half-expected every living thing to be up there celebrating his good news. *Ululululu!*

Only the pale English sun-ball hung low in the sky. The breeze raised goose bumps on his bare legs. There were no birds.

Flambeau sucked in the sun's scant heat and was quiet.

He was hunter enough to wait.

It didn't take long for a fat London pigeon to land on the half-wall and strut its meat and bones in front of the boy.

But Flambeau didn't want a pigeon. He wanted an *Intunguru*, the dusky turtle dove found in the forest around Bukavu. He knew the closest he could get in this vast city was its collared cousin.

Flambeau's irises hardened to pinpricks when he saw the slender brown bird with the black gash on the back of its neck flutter first onto the gutter of the boiler room and then onto the half-wall.

The boy took the catty out of his back pocket and crept towards the dove.

The creature's eyes rolled in alarm at his approach.

Flambeau stopped. He made a sound in the back of his throat, '*Prrt, tsu tsu tsu.*'

The bird ducked its head, mollified. Its answering call was a mellifluous '*CooCOOcoo*'.

Flambeau smiled, 'Ah.' And then mimicked the bird exactly, '*CooCOOcoo.*'

Then Flambeau began to sing.

He would never have done that if he had known he was not alone. He didn't see the gangly young woman in the shadow of the chimney, freckled belly pale in the gap between the top of her too-big jeans and her T-shirt.

Her name was Eleanor.

It took Eleanor a moment to realise Flambeau was singing to the bird.

It was bare-boned music. The notes hung in the air as if the longing inside the boy made its way to the outside when he sang. It had the power to make the dove go completely still and turn to face him as if to say *kill me now*.

Poor creature. It didn't clock the catty in Flambeau's hand. Or the small muscles in his back bound up tighter than a telephone wire.

The child was so still, even as he sang, that Eleanor swore she could hear his blood pump and see the rush of it under his skin.

He wanted that bird.

Whiz, thwack, and the stone hit home. Eleanor cried out. Flambeau whipped around to see her staring at him, wide-eyed. It was hard to say who was the more surprised.

Neither of them had the faintest chance of escape from the dilated gaze of the other – not the voyeur, nor the poacher. They blinked at one another.

Her freckles and the steadiness of her bright blue gaze made Flambeau think of water. He grinned, a dazzling show of white teeth.

'What you kill the pigeon for?' she asked.

'It's not a pigeon,' he said. 'It's a dove.'

'Why'd you kill it?'

'For my mama,' said the boy and he looked at her. Eleanor saw the sun rise up in his face when he said that.

'For her to eat,' he continued. 'When she comes.'

It had been five months since Flambeau's mother had tricked him into leaving Bukavu with the promise that she would follow swiftly on.

Being away from her had felt like being burned in a fire. Every day the flames licked at his feet and the coals burned his hands.

Her name was Bijou. Flambeau thought it the perfect name for his mother because she was, indeed, a jewel.

He didn't want to imagine the journey Bijou was now finally making from the forests of south-east Congo because he knew the pitfalls in her path were plentiful. So he didn't.

He just imagined laying a platter of slowly roasted birds on the table in front of her when she arrived. He imagined the way she would hold the small bones with her fingertips and how delicately she would pick the flesh off with her teeth. He could see the juice drip down her chin before she laughed and wiped it away.

He could feel the spit fill his mouth in readiness for the taste.

Eleanor began to turn away.

'I'm Flambeau,' said the boy.

She stopped. You didn't meet someone called that everyday. She turned back and said, 'Hello . . . Flambeau.'

She could see that he was waiting for her to offer her name in return, but she didn't say it because she hated it. She had always wanted to be a Charlotte or a Sophie but had been christened Eleanor after her mother, and thereby doomed to a life of mediocrity.

Flambeau wasn't mediocre.

Eleanor knew, without asking, that he was Congolese. Just like her boyfriend, Knight. He was another one with a name worth having. Knight. Oh, and he was true to its meaning, inside and out.

It seemed to Eleanor that the streets of London parted for Knight just as the Red Sea had for Moses. She didn't know how he had put ten lifetimes' worth of living into his twenty-eight years, but he had. She, on the other hand, was nineteen and still rattled at being alive.

There was nothing in her childhood in the far north of Scotland to prepare her for Tottenham High Street in the East End of London.

When she went to the Queen's Street Market for the first time it seemed to her like a new country. There wasn't a native Englishman for miles, apart from the fishmonger, a city-born pretender who could neither fillet a fish nor scale it.

Then she saw Knight.

He wore a wide, red cowboy hat. He didn't just buy a fish, he haggled, he bartered and he flirted. When he leaned across the plastic tubs of eel and red snapper to collect his pound of smoked hake for less than half the asking price, he softened the blow with a laugh. An exploding-bomb laugh that shook a smile out of the fishmonger's recalcitrant English soul even though he knew he'd been robbed.

Eleanor heard that laugh for a long time after. Just as she would hear Flambeau's song after he had packed up and gone home for the night.

It was mysterious to her how Flambeau's song and Knight's laugh eased the pain of their respective prey. Certainly, the dove's death would have been downright banal otherwise. She found herself thinking that at least it was crooned at before it was gone.

Flambeau peered off the roof to see where the dove corpse had landed when the door to the roof burst open behind him and Eugene stormed in screaming blue murder. He wanted the savage who had killed his bird.

Eugene kept pigeons, along with finches and a swift or two, in the cage on the roof. He told everyone who would listen that he saw himself as East London's answer to Saint Francis of Assisi. He even had the ponytail, only his crop of hair was thin and oily and speckled with grey. Eleanor thought he was grey-skinned too, in the way only a long-term Londoner can be.

She smiled to herself when she thought about Saint Eugene eating breakfast on his veranda when *fleep* – there was a dead bird looking up at him from the middle of his yoke.

'Had to be one of these little fuckers,' he crowed when he saw Flambeau frozen on the roof with his catty in hand.

'It's not a pigeon!' blurted Flambeau.

'Look at the bird, Eugene,' snapped Eleanor.

He did as she instructed.

'Is it one of yours?'

Eugene reluctantly shook his head.

'Right then,' she said.

That didn't stop him raging. Flambeau listened to Eugene's bluster about the 'scum' moving onto the estate from all over creation. The child didn't need to know what scum meant to know it did not bode well for him. He could hear that in the sound of the word.

Flambeau slipped behind Eleanor for protection. He fitted himself so completely into the shape of her slim body that he was entirely hidden from Eugene's view. Still, he felt the heat of the Londoner's wrath. So he crept silently closer to Eleanor until he could smell her hair. It smelt like the sea. He sank down behind her legs and prayed for the diatribe to come to an end.

At the peak of his outrage Eugene insisted Flambeau show his face. The boy duly emerged from Eleanor's shadow and Eugene extracted a promise from him that he would forget his brutal African ways and never kill another bird.

Flambeau whispered, 'I swear.'

But even as he said it he knew it wasn't true. For his mother, he would roast every bird in London, whatever Eugene said.

Flambeau set to work as soon as Eugene had gone back to his bacon and eggs. 'CooCOOcoo, cooCOOcoo,' he called. And the doves came.

It wasn't long before he had a half-filled Tesco bag full of corpses. When he held up the bag to show Eleanor she clapped like a madwoman.

Watching Flambeau hunt was like seeing nature and boy come together to put on the perfect show. That didn't happen to every kid on the block. It was magic.

Flambeau picked a dead bird out of the packet, handed it to Eleanor as a thank-you gift and said, 'Fat.'

It was a juicy word, and he smiled as he said it again, 'Fat!'

His smile was like the scent flowers give out to attract bees.

Eleanor didn't know it then, but the doves were not Flambeau's only conquest that day. It was her heart that was the real prize, and he now held it in his small brown hand.

# *Tomorrow*

Flambeau's Aunt Laetitia didn't think he was magic. To her he was one more mouth to feed. The boy didn't have an easy time in her house. Ever. But that evening was one of the worst.

The first thing his Uncle Didier did was throw his collared doves into the bin. Did Flambeau think they were farm people? In London you don't eat wild birds.

Flambeau knew his Uncle Didier was hungry. He was always hungry, but still he wouldn't eat a dove in case someone thought less of him for his rural African ways. That can easily make a good man cruel.

All Flambeau could do was look at his bagful of treasures as it lay half-in, half-out of the tall silver dustbin with the foot-operated lid. If he squeezed his eyes half shut it seemed as if the bird nearest to the top was going to make a run for it.

When Aunt Laetitia came home with a Tesco chicken for Bijou's welcome feast, Didier said she was putting on airs. There was no pleasing him. You would have thought he would be happy that Flambeau's mother was about to come and take the child off his hands. But he was not.

Maybe he liked the power he had over the boy? Or perhaps he planned on putting him to work? Sometimes Flambeau caught his uncle looking at him as if searching for someone else in his face. He wondered idly if it were Bijou his uncle longed to see there. He would not be the first.

Flambeau and his five cousins shared a small bedroom meant for two. Most nights he fell asleep listening to his uncle and aunt fight about whether to buy palm oil or smoked fish. They could not have both, even though both were essential for a good Congolese pondu.

If they had been in Bukavu they could have walked into the fields and picked some wild spinach or traded something with a neighbour. But you couldn't do that when your neighbour was Saint Eugene.

In London, Flambeau noticed, what would have been enough anywhere else felt like too little. Although he did not see the rags and swollen-belly poverty of his home country, the open jaws of the empty food cupboard promised equal suffering, particularly when half the week was still ahead of them.

His aunt said the government stipend that kept starvation from the door could be taken away *just like that*, and she snapped her fingers to show him how mercurial fate could be. Flambeau could see how the uncertainty of it all pitted his uncle and aunt against one another. Even their occasional lovemaking sounded to him more like fury and grief than tenderness.

On those nights, Flambeau did his best to stuff his ears with toilet paper and pray for his mother to come quickly. He prayed ardently.

The family attended the makeshift church just across the road from the railway station. It was an Anglican church during the morning and became an evangelical place of worship in the afternoons and evenings. There, for a few hours twice a week, they were elevated out of the mire to bask in the rays of God's love.

Flambeau took reluctant leave of his doves, half-in and half-out of the silver dustbin, and went to wait at the doors of the church even before they opened for the evening service. He chose a seat right in the front where he could better implore the Virgin to watch over his mother as she travelled the final miles of her journey to him.

The pastor wore Versace silk. He had a gold tooth, which flashed as he spoke of the place God kept for them-all in heaven, free of the suffering they endured on earth. In his rolling African French he brought his congregation, incrementally, phrase by phrase, to their feet.

His deep baritone could have paved the way to heaven when he sang. The backing trio were as good as the Pointer Sisters, just more beautiful, wound up as they were in African cloth. Even Aunt Laetitia at the drum machine was no longer matronly but rather humming with rhythm and beat.

The whole congregation joined in for the chorus, and collectively they all sang open the golden gates. You've never seen so many beautiful people shining in such fervent communion. It had to bode well for Flambeau's mother.

Flambeau prayed that no one would trick her the way she had tricked him. That would not be fair.

Bitter saliva filled his mouth when he remembered the day in Bukavu market when she had handed him over to the man in the black hat.

If you are nine years old and sweating in the fierce equatorial heat, a popsicle is what you want more than anything on earth. That frozen liquid sugar, dyed bright red or orange or luminous green.

Flambeau had chosen green. He was so close to bliss as the sweet hit his tongue that he didn't see his mother bent in heated conversation with the skinny man in the black hat.

Later, he cursed himself for not paying attention because he could have made a run for it when he saw her hand over the wad of money. But that was just brave talk. How would he have known then that she was paying the skinny man to take her son from Bukavu to London with not even a passport to ease the way?

Anyway, he didn't notice. He hardly noticed when his ma turned and ran through the crowded bus station without a backward glance. He wouldn't have known why she did that. Much later he understood that she had to run before her love for him made her grab him back and hold him to her chest and moan.

When he finally did heed that she was leaving, he wondered if she was playing a game. He remembered the feeling of the half-formed laugh on his lips as he started to follow her.

That was when the skinny man picked him up, kicking and screaming, dumped him in the back of the pick-up truck parked on the corner, and drove out of town.

By the time Flambeau's long journey came to an end he wasn't kicking and screaming any more.

When they got home from church Laetitia served the children's food on one large plate. '*We call on your blood to purify this meagre food, from any ills . . . in the name of the Lord Jesus. Amen,*' said Didier.

And the children echoed him, '*Amen, Amen, Amen.*'

Flambeau waited for a chance to reach in and take a marble-sized ball of fufu and dip it into the small bowl of leftover manioc leaf and onion pondu but it didn't come. When he stretched out his hand for the dish, it moved just out of his reach. He tried again, and again it moved.

It was the same every night. He wanted to shout at them, to shame them for their selfishness, but he did not dare open his mouth for fear of ridicule.

When he first arrived in London, Flambeau found his cousins and his immigrant classmates ashamed of their family's foreignness.

They went around sounding more London than the Londoners, saying things like, 'Fuck me, she's a bitch now, *innit*?' And, 'You get nicked for that, freak.'

'What you say, freak?'

'I say you a freak, freak.'

Then they would point and say, 'He's the freak.'

'Who?'

'Flambeau.'

So the boy shut his mouth.

At first he looked to his schoolteacher, the Australian Miss Glenys, for help with his English. But come the end of the second week Miss Glenys laid her head on the desk and wept in despair at the intransigence of her pupils.

Flambeau worked silently and alone to master the language so he wouldn't be the freak any more.

It was a ferocious process and deeply eremitic. He was consumed by it. Like the donkey carcass he and his mother had once seen on the side of the road in Bukavu. It was as if he had crawled inside its ribcage with a clamour of words and sewn the skin shut.

That is where he remained until Miss Glenys took them to the park to celebrate the end of their second term of school.

It was the day his classmate Ayesha was mauled by a Staffordshire bull terrier, and Flambeau spoke his first full sentence in the Queen's English.

Even then, he would probably not have done so if he'd had a choice. Miss Glenys was pink-faced with distress when she insisted that Flambeau report what he had seen of the dog incident.

He opened his mouth and said, carefully, 'The man with the dog said Ayesha looked like the grim reaper in her bloody Muslin burkha. And that's why the dog went for her.'

He said the word Muslim as if it was the fabric and not the faith: *Muslin*.

Miss Glenys looked as if she wanted to slap Flambeau's face. He could see she had confused the dog-owner's sentiment with his own, but he didn't have the courage to correct her.

When the man and his dog sauntered past them a few minutes later, the hapless Miss Glenys didn't open her mouth to protest his bigotry or his animal's viciousness.

Flambeau wondered if his uncle would be kinder to him if he had a Staffordshire bull terrier at his side?

Flambeau kicked out hard under the table.

His cousins wailed. Didier was out of his seat in a flash and thwacked all five heads, one by one, very fast.

'*Enough!*' he hissed, eyes dangerously bright.

Flambeau was still achingly hungry as he lay on the mattress on the floor in the tiny bedroom. Bunk beds on either side of him held his sleeping cousins.

He listened to his uncle and aunt preparing for bed next door. It was clear to him that the rising volume of their conversation was going to lead to another night of lust and grief. Flambeau couldn't bear to hear his aunt call out and then weep into her pillow even though he knew this would be the last time. His mother would make sure of that. One look at how he lived here and she would hold him to her chest and say, '*Never again.*'

Flambeau crept out of bed. He walked silently to the bursting-at-the-seams dustbin that held his bag of birds, pulled them out and headed for the roof.

Aaah, the wide-open range of the roof. The low clouds, made orange by reflected London streetlights, drifted close over his head. He sucked in the air. He saw the shape of a person on the edge of the roof. He called softly, 'Hello?'

She answered, 'Hello.'

'Who's there?' he asked.

When she turned he recognised the redhead who had saved him from Eugene and wondered if she was often there, sitting quietly in the dark.

'You going to cook those?' She pointed to his packet of birds.

He thought about it for a moment and then said, 'They forbid it.'

'Who does?' she asked.

'Them.' He meant Didier and Laetitia, but he wasn't going to describe their cruelties for fear of driving away his new friend.

'What's your name?' he asked.

She hesitated and then said, 'Eleanor.'

'Hello, Eleanor.'

She smiled.

Flambeau opened the door of Eugene's birdcage, held his breath so as not to disturb its occupants, and sat on a cardboard box in the corner. His '*prrt, tsu tsu tsu*' calmed the finches and pigeons.

The boy cradled the packet of dead birds on his lap. He was quiet for a moment. It was the kind of quiet that is brimful of cerebration, as if he was calculating a difficult equation. Then he said, as if willing it, 'We're going away, me and Mama.'

'Oh?'

'Somewhere far. And very hot.'

She murmured, 'Well, I hope you have better luck doing that than I have.'

Eleanor glanced down at the stream of lights on the high street below. It looked like a river, flowing, pausing, then flowing again. Knight was one of those lights. She tried to pick out his shape in the crowds below.

Knight had promised to take Eleanor away many times. First to Rome, then Budapest and Paris. He'd been saying so for nearly six months.

He was wearing the same red cowboy hat the day she started work at the minicab office. He and a couple of friends rented a small room in the back of the minicab place, which they called their office.

From there, they ran their affairs and made a sport of seeing the new cab controllers crash and burn on their first day.

Londoners can be brutal when they sense someone on the line who may not know one end of the city from the other. The melodic tones of Eleanor's very rural Scottish accent and her inability to tell Mill Lane from Mill Hill or Mill Terrace or Mill-bloody-Walk were a dead giveaway.

She heard her dad's voice inside her head as she tried to get it straight. He said, 'Sink or swim, lass.' So instead of cursing like a swine and beating her head on the desk she stuck her hair up with a pencil and decided to give as good as she got.

She said 'Have a good day now' to as many people as she could before they slammed the phone down on her. It became a game to pass the hours and ease the shame of not knowing where in the world anyone wanted to go.

When Knight leaned over the counter at the end of the day and said, 'I want a taxi and I want you in it,' her head shot up. She would have gone to China in a paper boat for the way his look made her feel.

It filled her belly with heat. She could not have said it then but later she understood that it was her hunger that he had roused.

The truth was Eleanor couldn't go away without Knight because he had stolen her heart and to keep breathing she had to stay close. When she told Flambeau that, all he said was, 'Oh.'

What else could the boy say but, 'Oh.'

Knight was the only thing Eleanor had ever wanted. Wanted so that she reached out and took without thinking. She showed him the entrance and she waved him inside. That made her a sitting duck forever after.

In spite of all that followed, she still said *hallelujah* when she remembered that, because somehow with him she was more than an Eleanor. She was a *chérie*.

Eleanor watched Flambeau take a dead bird from his plastic bag and lay it on the ground in the birdcage. She shook her head and told him that Sally was a lost cause. He looked up at her. 'You know Sally?'

She held up two fingers and said, 'Me and her are well tight.'

Flambeau smiled at her and shook the bird a little bit. That small animal movement galvanised the snake and she emerged from the darkness under his feet.

Eleanor sucked in a breath when Sally rolled out because you can never be indifferent to the sight of a whopping great constrictor coming your way. 'Hello, Sally,' she whispered.

They both watched the snake slither over to the bird and take a sniff. She was one of Saint Eugene's menagerie of creatures. He had her teeth taken out in case she bit him and he fed her chicken and liver cat food forever after.

It occurred to Flambeau then that he could give Sally a shot at being a proper snake. He grew up with them all around him in the forest after all. He caught grass snakes and kept them in a box under his bed in Bukavu.

He also had two fang marks in his calf from a more unexpected encounter but he never held that against Sally.

The snake raised her head to watch as he began to pluck the feathers off the pigeon. He worked quickly and soon the bird was bare.

Flambeau and Eleanor laughed when Sally nudged the bird corpse with her snout. Then she stretched open her mouth and began to swallow it whole.

By the time it began its journey down her body like the knot in a rope, they were shrieking with pleasure.

The boy sent handfuls of feathers up into the sky in celebration. As they came down again he closed his eyes to better feel their soft arrival onto his cheeks and hair and eyelashes.

Some feathers never came back, but continued their journey upwards towards the skidding orange clouds. Tomorrow, Bijou the jewel would be there. Tomorrow.

# *Bijou*

Flambeau was up before it was properly light. He adjusted his school tie and shone his shoes with rolled-up newspaper until he could see his face in them. His mama liked shiny shoes.

There was not much traffic out that early. A lone car turned into the housing estate. Flambeau ran to look in the window. His heart ached in anticipation. Like someone had kicked him in his chest. A small dog jumped against the glass and barked. Not his mother. Not yet.

His cousins walked past on their way to school. They were like ground birds in their black school uniforms and all bunched together. Flambeau caught a glimpse of their feet, not human but webbed. Shuffling. They squawked rather than talked. It made him laugh. Today they couldn't touch him.

In Bukavu he had often lingered in the morning warmth of his blankets and listened to his mother laugh in the yard outside. She sounded like a hornbill calling – *kaaakakakaka*.

Back then Flambeau wasn't sure he liked its brazenly vivacious sound. *Kaaakakakaka*. It rocked his even keel.

Now he couldn't live without it. Today he would hear it again. Then they would dance the Rhumba. It was their dance.

He hadn't ever 'learnt' the Rhumba, not the way he learnt English or the times tables. He just took his mama's hand and she led him there.

His mama told him it was slaves who took the Rhumba from Africa and spread it around the world. When it came back home again it carried the beat of the Cubans it had encountered on its way, *one . . . three, four, one . . . three four.*

There it was! *Calling him.* That same beat. Flambeau followed the sound to the corner of the street. He saw an African man washing his blue car on the open concourse of the estate as Rhumba dance music blasted from his car stereo.

Flambeau didn't need anyone to tell him that this was Knight. Added to the wonder of the music were his shiny black trousers and smart snakeskin shoes.

Flambeau never dreamt that he would find someone here who loved the Rhumba like he and his mama did. But there he was, moving to the beat as he worked.

Flambeau could not help but do the same. Before he knew it he had shimmied into the stairwell where he thought no one could see him. As he danced he watched Knight rinse the soap off the car with a hosepipe until every bubble was gone.

When Eleanor turned up with a pink bucket of hot soapy water to wash the wheel rims, Knight stopped his labour and they kissed.

Flambeau slowed his dancing to watch, even though it seemed to him that he shouldn't be there. He meant to turn away.

He saw Knight envelope Eleanor like a thick vine, part lover and part constrictor. Then the Congolese charmer led his love seamlessly into a Rhumba, slightly ironic but very skilled: *one . . . three, four, one . . . three four.*

When Knight caught sight of Flambeau hiding in the stairwell he winked at him as if to say *she can't be what she is not*. And then he smiled as if the child's stolen presence there was the most natural thing in the world.

Flambeau saw that Eleanor was not a great dancer.

That didn't stop her trying. He watched Knight and Eleanor dance until the water from the forgotten hosepipe flowed over Knight's snakeskin shoes and he stopped to dry them lovingly with an ink-blue silk handkerchief he pulled from his inside jacket pocket.

As Eleanor turned off the tap she too saw the boy hovering in the stairwell and shouted, 'Flambeau! Come and meet my Knight,' and she waved him over.

Flambeau shook Knight's hand deferentially as he had been raised to do with an elder. '*I greet you, father.*'

Knight cocked his head at the child's staid Lingala. Underneath he could hear the Swahili of the south-east as well as another more mysterious rhythm. He listened as Flambeau repeated his greeting and then he got it. The boy spoke Lingala with the cadence of the Banyamulengu. Knight had not heard this Kinyarwanda for a long time, and he knew the people who spoke it had seen dark times.

He countered its sobriety with his own Kinshasa patois. '*I'm sweet, homeboy. Sweet like sugar.*'

A smile burst through Flambeau's shyness and he blurted, '*Me too!*'

'Oh?'

'My mother is coming today.'

'*From Kinshasa?*' asked Knight.

Flambeau nodded, grinning. Knight saw his excitement, 'Ah,' he said, '*that* is *sweet.*'

Knight leaned on his car door, turned up the volume on his music system and asked, '*You know this band?*'

Flambeau shook his head.

Knight turned the volume up still further and said, '*Listen and tell me who it is.*'

Flambeau's eyes shone at the challenge. Knight egged him on. '*Come on. Take a shot.*'

A grin flitted across Flambeau's face as he guessed. '*Maison Mère?*'

It was Knight's turn to laugh. '*Try again.*'

'*Olomide?*'

'*Aaah no. Again. Think now. Think!*'

Flambeau listened, head bowed, then he shouted, '*Kekele!*'

'*Yeees-sa-sa.*' Knight laughed that exploding-bomb laugh and took a couple of notes from his wallet.

Flambeau took the money gingerly. A pause between the music tracks brought unexpected gravity to the exchange. Then a voice ripped through the quiet like the shriek of a jackal. '*Haai. Keep away from that boy. You rubbish.*'

All three of them turned to see Aunt Laetitia on the balcony three floors up.

Even at this distance Flambeau could see it was one of her bad days. Still in her pyjamas in the middle of the morning, with her headscarf crooked on her head. She seemed to have forgotten herself, let alone the imminent arrival of Flambeau's mother.

'*Look at those fancy shoes,*' she screamed at Knight. '*Where you get those shoes? Hey?*'

Flambeau wanted to shout right back at her, '*And you? Look at you. You want Mama to see you standing there howling like a madwoman in your pyjamas?*' Even though he did not dare open his mouth his thoughts continued in that vein.

*Couldn't she see that Knight always wore fancy shoes? He was a Sapeur.*
*Even a country boy like him knew a Sapeur when he saw one.*

Then and there, trapped in the no-man's-land between the shining
Sapeur and the haggard woman on the balcony, the boy made his
choice. His vowed silently to himself that he would become Knight's
apprentice and join the ranks of *La Société des Ambianceurs et des Personnes*
*Elégantes* forever.

Flambeau was no fool.

Knight and the Sapeurs understood the importance of beauty to
the business of survival. To dress this way gave them a kind of disguise.
The more trauma and hardship they had lived through, the more there
was to hide and the more style was needed to hide it.

They were pacifists from a country that had seen much war and at
best their beauty spoke of the depth of their determination not to be
destroyed by life's cruelties.

Papa Wemba, that bright star in the firmament of Congolese Rhumba
music, was their founder and their deity.

Being a Sapeur meant that Knight would never appear in his pyjamas
with a scarf lopsided on his head. He would never frighten his dear
ones with the uncomfortable facts of his condition. The dandy in him
would dodge the traumatised, cash-strapped immigrant that waited
for him always. It was his private matter, to be dealt with alone, in
the dark pit of the night.

Flambeau could see that Laetitia could never achieve this degree of
invention and that she hated all Sapeurs for being able to pull it off.
'*They buy-buy-buy, these Kinshasa gangsters, but they don't work. Now you*
*tell me how that can be?*' she shouted.

Flambeau looked at Knight and mumbled his apology. '*Sorry.*'

Knight shrugged. Eleanor continued to roll up the hose and asked, 'What's her beef, Flambeau?'

'She doesn't like his shoes,' mumbled the boy.

Eleanor looked at Knight and smiled. 'I wouldn't get between him and those shoes if I were her.'

'She's just jealous,' Flambeau said, by way of comfort and illumination.

'Thank you,' murmured Knight.

Flambeau carefully folded the notes Knight had given him and was stuffing them in his pocket when Laetitia turned her wrath on him. '*That money in your hand is other people's money, my boy.*' And then she raised the stakes. '*Now give it back.*'

The money was a gift. It was his. Flambeau churned.

'*Now. Give it back NOW,*' she screeched.

Flambeau slowly unfolded the notes and held them out to Knight.

Knight made a show of taking the money but slipped the notes back into Flambeau's pocket as he passed. '*Put it in your shoe. She won't look there,*' he murmured.

It occurred to Flambeau that even his own blood father would not have been so tuned in to him, so silently and generously in his corner. He whispered, '*Thank you.*'

'*Now get away from that crook,*' shrieked Laetitia, '*Right now. Right bloody now.*'

Knight turned up the volume of the music to drown her out.

The boy surreptitiously stuffed the money into the side of his shoe and turned to walk away from Knight, crippled with reluctance.

It was midday by the time Eugene tracked Flambeau down to his street corner. He didn't say a word at first but stood beside him. Both of them peered into the passing car windows, heads moving almost in time. They made a pretty strange twosome: glowing African child and squalid urban hippie.

Flambeau sounded a little subdued when he said, 'My mother is coming today.'

'That right?' said Eugene.

Eugene wore sandals. Flambeau had never seen bare English feet before. To him they weren't feet, they were loaves of pale, recently risen bread slapped down on the leather plate of the sandal.

Flambeau knew from the way they were shaped that those feet had never run along a dirt path in the forest, nor carried the weight of a bag of ground cassava to the market.

Eugene was there to tell the boy that Sally ate cat food, not birds. He said that there were enough feathers in her cage to stuff a bloody mattress. 'They could get stuck in her throat, you know.'

Flambeau looked up at him and said, 'What?'

Then Eugene said, 'The feathers.'

'Oh,' said Flambeau, and he turned away. He turned back when a new thought came to him. 'They come out after the rain, you know.'

'What does?' asked Eugene.

'Snakes.'

They like to slither through the wet. The dog-eared snake book in the clinic in Bukavu had a picture of a snake with its fangs bared. Underneath it were the words *Western Barred Spitting Cobra or Naja nigricollis*.

It had just rained the day *Naja nigricollis* waited for Flambeau on the dark red soil of the forest. It bit him twice. He couldn't smell the honeysuckle on his mother's skin for a year after that.

His father ran the half-mile to the clinic with Flambeau in his arms. As the child lay on the dirty floor among the sick and war-wounded he put his hand inside his mother's shirt. He put his hand against her breast to feel the heartbeat under her skin.

The flying ants came out after dark in swarms and immolated themselves on the candles lighting the clinic. When he heard his mother talk about it later she called that night *la nuit d'apocalypse*.

When the pain in his massively swollen leg woke him three hours later, his hand was still there against his mother's breast and she was asleep beside him.

He withdrew it as if he had been stung. He blushed. A surge of hate for her swept through him. He was almost a man. Didn't she know that? What if his father, keeping vigil there in the doorway of the clinic, had seen his childish need?

She must have felt his rage but when his eyes rolled back into his head a short time later it was his mother who sang them back into their sockets.

There was still no sign of Bijou by late afternoon. Flambeau was half starved and burnt a darker shade of brown by the sun. His creeping sense of dread made the time pass like slowly melting wax, invisibly.

The child was drained almost to nothing when he saw the solitary woman making her way up the hill towards him. He rose to his feet. The luminous pink glow of the summer evening made her lovely as she laboured up the hill with her suitcase.

He moved towards her. Tentative. Then bolder. It was her!

He started to run. It was going to be all right.

He ran like a madman. As he got closer, the delight on his face faltered.

The woman's feet were covered with newspaper.

He stopped. What looked like a scarf around her head from a distance was a shopping bag.

His breath stopped in his throat when she lifted her head to reveal a face puffed and blue from who-knows-what abuse.

And she didn't even know he was there as she shuffled past, leaving him gutted in her wake.


Flambeau didn't see the dusk coming, so curled in on himself was he. He heard someone call his name. It was a gentle sound but not his mother's voice, so he didn't lift his head. It came again.

'Flambeau.'

This time he looked up. Laetitia stood on the corner, bathed clean and dressed in her best. She gestured to him to come. '*Everything is ready*,' she said.

He nodded. But he would not leave his post.

His aunt didn't seem to want to go either. This was not the harridan of the morning. Flambeau didn't fully understand or trust the change in her, but they were allies in wanting the reunion with his mother, and he would forgive most things for that.

He still wondered in his acute, ten-year-old way if his aunt was sorry for having loved him so poorly. Perhaps she feared that his mother would see how it was for him in her home and rage against her sister for failing him thus. Certainly, her face had a tentative eagerness he had not seen before.

He was not moved. 'I will show my mother the way when she arrives,' he said, claiming the more profound relationship to her and to the task of seeing her home. He enjoyed the power it gave him.

Laetitia hesitated for a moment then nodded her head and turned to walk away.

Darkness did not bring with it a cooling of the day. It seemed to trap the heat and add pressure until the night hummed with it. Thick traffic flowed up and down the hill.

It was not often that Flambeau found himself on London's streets after dark. He more often sought the solace of the roof when the light faded. Now he found his despair replaced by fluttering anxiety at the mysterious movement he saw in the darkness beyond the road.

Flambeau sprang to his feet just as a huge truck bore down on him, its headlights burning, blinding coals. Flambeau scrambled to escape their puissance, turned on his heels and ran. He raced across the wide, deserted open concourse and pounded up five flights of stairs until the air tore painfully in and out of his chest.

He ran straight into the eye of a storm.


'*You will not touch it!*' Aunt Laetitia stood at the head of the table laid for a feast: roast chicken, pondu and cassava. Flambeau watched his cousins and their father mill around the table, hyena-like.

Uncle Didier snapped at his wife, '*You want us to watch it grow mould?*'

'*It is for my sister,*' she cried.

Didier shouted, '*Your sister is not coming.*'

'*Liar!*' Fierce tears ran down Flambeau's cheeks as he shouted, '*You bastard liar.*'

Everyone stopped to look.

Didier turned slowly.

Flambeau faced his uncle and spoke more quietly. '*I don't have my birds any more,*' his voice shook. '*If you eat the chicken, my mother will have no food after her long journey.*'

The cousins huddled together like lemmings in response to the violence in the air. Flambeau looked from one adult face to the other, desperate to read their intentions.

'*I'm going to phone the police*,' said Laetitia in an unsteady voice.

'*And tell them what?*' snapped Didier.

She turned to look at him. Didier bent his body in a caricature of servitude and rubbed his hands together. '*Please, Mr Policeman, can you find my sister? A trafficker brought her to London and now she has* . . . (he blew on his fingers) . . . *poof.*'

Laetitia looked away. '*Don't speak that way, Didier.*'

'*What way?*' Didier turned, neck taut, eyes wide, a giant bird poised to strike. '*This way?*' and he swept the mountain of official papers off the sideboard and onto the floor.

Laetitia got down on her knees and began to pick them up.

Didier looked down at his wife, he shook his head and hissed, '*There's a coffin waiting for you in Bukavu, Laetitia.*'

The youngest of the cousins began to cry.

'*It's made of cardboard* . . . *and it's waiting for you. You and your Banyamulengu children,*' said Didier.

Laetitia looked at him. If the children had not been there she would have spat in his eye.

Didier barked, '*Now, carve the chicken.*' And he picked up the crying child.

Flambeau held his breath. What was she going to do?

He watched his aunt slowly take up the carving knife. She sliced into the bird. That was enough for him – he headed for the door.

But Didier was there in his path. His uncle said, '*Sit.*'

Flambeau looked at him.

Didier was very still even when he spoke. '*This family is going to eat now.*'

A plate laden with a feast of cassava, pondu and chicken was set in front of Flambeau. Didier's voice sounded very far away when he said, '*Eat.*'

'*Eat.*'

Flambeau picked up a drumstick and took a bite. He chewed with tears and snot pouring down his face.

# Dark Night

'*Eish. Bad things happen in this world, my child,*' was all Laetitia said to Flambeau as she turned out his light.

The moment his aunt had closed the door Flambeau wrapped his belt around his wrist and tied it to the burglar bars of the window. It would catch him if he fell asleep. He was going to wait for his mother. He would be there to sing out her name and open the door when he heard her footsteps coming up the stairs.

He woke at dawn with his wrist blue and his body slumped halfway down the wall. There had been no footsteps.

His cousins once again passed Flambeau as he waited on the pavement.

This morning they chanted in London-speak, '*She's dead, innit? Your mother's dead, freak.*' Then scattered like leaves when he lunged for them.

He could hear their laughter long after they had gone. The sound swept across him again and again. It left behind sharp, hard ridges on his breaking heart like the wind does when it stirs up desert sand.

★

Flambeau didn't even look up when the blue car purred to a stop on the street in front of him.

'*You know this voice?*' asked Knight, and hit the play button.

Flambeau said nothing. Knight turned up the volume. Flambeau was silent still.

Knight got out of his car and crouched down in front of Flambeau. The boy still did not look up.

'*Take a shot,*' he said.

You could hardly hear Flambeau when he whispered, '*Papa Wemba?*'

Knight howled in derision. He cupped his ear and mock-listened, '*What you say?*'

Flambeau tried again. '*Mwalimu?*'

Knight hit his knees. '*Homeboy . . . what are you thinking?*'

Flambeau looked at Knight and said, '*Stupid old stuff whatever it is.*'

'*Old stuff? And you say you love Congo music?*' he howled.

Flambeau reared up and pushed Knight off the pavement with a sharp thrust, '*More than you do. Much more.*'

Flambeau really wanted to call Knight a blood-sucking bastard, he wanted to call him a fucking, pissing pig. He wanted to hate him because he could see that not even he and his music could make things better.

'*Haai, haai, haai,*' said Knight. '*If you love Congo music then get down and pray at the altar of Joseph – Kabasele – Tshamala!*'

The boy's face cracked.

Where Knight had hoped for a smile he saw downright devastation. Oh Jesus!

And then the boy muttered, '*My mama's favourite.*'

Knight saw a dark shadow engulf Flambeau entirely and he understood.

'*Your mama did not come,*' he whispered.

No. She did not come.

The dark engulfed Knight then too. He knew that when a woman went missing it was never a good thing.

Knight and Flambeau sat on the pavement in silence. Joseph Kabasele's melancholy tune spun a web about their grief. They were suspended in its strange succour for a moment.

They saw the shape of a cat streak under the body of his car and peer out at them from the shadows.

'*My mama and I knew a cat like that,*' Knight said. '*It moved into our shack one day when it was raining. Just walked in from the street there in Ndjili like it was his place.*' He laughed softly.

Flambeau looked up at him.

Knight seized on this glimmer of interest and continued, '*My mother named him Suffering.*'

'*Suffering?*' asked Flambeau, almost inaudibly.

Knight nodded. He told Flambeau he was grateful to Suffering because the cat had lain on his mother's bony chest and the thin rumble of its purring and the scant warmth of its body comforted his mother as she lay.

Knight touched his chest to mark the place where the cat had lain and said, '*If Suffering was here when I opened my eyes in the morning I knew Mama was still breathing.*'

Flambeau considered this, his head down. Then he said quietly, '*It is a good name for the cat of a sick person.*'

'Yes,' said Knight.

Eleanor walked across the wide, black-tarred concourse of the housing estate. Early-morning mist near the damp part of the estate made her passage ephemeral. It was how she felt, half-there, as if her sleepless night had prepared only part of her for the day.

She took her place amongst the scattering of people waiting at the bus stop, and only then did she hear the Congo music as it snaked through the dense early-morning air to her ears. She turned and saw Knight and Flambeau, face to face on the pavement, still held rapt by Joseph Kabasele's beautiful voice.

She blinked. She had spent half the night waiting first for the boy, and then the man.

Whenever a door had banged on the roof she had turned in antici-pation, 'Flambeau?' But he had not come. Someone in amongst the river of lights below had shouted obscenities into the night, '. . . *did you just call me a prick?*'

Eleanor had sighed and eaten a spoonful of the cold baked beans she'd brought for Flambeau. The distant voice had continued, '*Hey . . . don't you fucking walk away when I'm talking to you . . .*'

She'd chewed the beans slowly and tried to shut out the rising anguish in the voice below. '*Jesus, Annie, just . . . wait. Wait for me . . .*'

Then she'd tipped the rest of the beans out into the empty flower-pot. Flambeau wasn't coming.

Waiting for Knight had been worse.

Because she *never* knew where he went, she wondered sometimes if the dangers she imagined for him were worse than those he actu-ally faced.

She cleaned the flat from top to bottom to quell her imaginings. She even wiped the inside of the bath with bleach and watched as the brown stains on the sides faded. She had seen her ma do that often enough when her dad went on a bender.

When she finally fell asleep, it felt as if some part of her remained alert, perpetually ready for bad news.

Maybe if she'd been older she might have dealt with the whole situation more philosophically, but she was nineteen and time moved slowly for her. It left generous room for fear.

Now, after one of the longest nights of her short life, there sat Knight, listening to music with his small friend as if all was right with the world.

A small eruption of feeling travelled up Eleanor's spine like a bullet and she shouted, 'Where the bloody hell have you been, Knight?'

Flambeau and Knight looked up at her in surprise. She blamed the shoes for her tumble, but it was the shared feeling on their faces that sent her over the cardboard box and flat on her face.

She looked at Knight from the grimy pavement. 'What time d'you think this is to come home, you bastard? I thought you were DEAD.'

She saw Flambeau start to cry but she couldn't stop to comfort him because she was lost herself.

She tore the high-heeled shoes off her feet. 'You can never be in a hurry if you wear shoes like this,' she said. 'Did you know that?'

Knight reached out his hand to help her to her feet but she simply slapped him out of the way. She took a shuddering breath and spat, 'I hate these shoes.'

Knight shook his head and smiled, 'But *chérie*, they make your legs go all the way to my heart.'

Knight turned to Flambeau and said conspiratorially, 'Dolce and Gabbana. Sloane Street.'

It was the Sapeur in him that made him say that.

Flambeau's eyes opened wide. He had not the slightest idea who Dolce and Gabbana were, but he knew they mattered, and he vowed to himself that he would find out.

Eleanor wanted to scream, 'Damn Dolce and Gabbana to hell.' But this time she didn't because she saw Knight turn to Flambeau and say, 'When your mama comes we will take her there and we will buy her a pair of shoes.'

Flambeau looked down at his hands. He jammed his lips together to stop them shaking. Couldn't say a word. Just shook his head.

She wasn't going to come.

Knight held his hand out to the boy. Flambeau's face was grave as he considered the new intimacy it offered. Then he reached out and took it.

Eleanor knew the quotidian terrors, losses and disappointments that are part of being an ordinary human. But Knight knew the Congo. Flambeau and Knight knew the worst.

And that's how come, just at the right moment, Knight knew to say, 'If she is lost . . .'

Flambeau looked up.

'. . . then you must find her.'

Those nine simple words brought a sliver of light into the murk and made the world start slowly turning again.

*Part Two*

# The Task

Knight's call to arms rang in Flambeau's head for the rest of the day. It marshalled his perilous passage from day to night without conflict with his uncle or his cousins and without succumbing to the ink-dense grief that stalked him. It was only when Flambeau stopped moving and lay down on his mattress that he wondered how he was going to achieve it.

He barely closed his eyes through that whole long night. He wasn't able to say, even afterwards, what it was he was busy with. If he had read the *Odyssey* he might have recognised the preparations he was making to his inner world, but his ma was saving that story for when he was older. It would have been better too for his mission if he had been older, because whenever he got to the *knowing what to do* part of his imagined road, he wept silent tears of helplessness. He did not know. Not even remotely.

As he lay in the stifling room surrounded by his sleeping cousins, he saw his mother, bent over the kitchen table in their house in Bukavu.

He saw his younger self, three or four years old, tug at her skirt to get her attention, but she simply raised her hand to silence him.

Even at that age he knew his mother only did this when she was doing her most serious work.

Flambeau dragged a chair to her side and climbed onto it to see what she was doing.

She was writing. The paper on the table in front of her was filling up with words. Each one stacked on top of the other until they looked like a ladder.

When Flambeau asked his mother why she was writing a ladder she laughed that *kakkakakaka* laugh of hers and said, '*It's not a ladder, it's a list.*' But it was a ladder, a Jacob's ladder of what to do next and the order in which to do it.

Flambeau crept past the sleeping bodies of his cousins and into the toilet because it was the only place he could turn on the light. There, on a torn piece of paper, he wrote the words:

> *boat*
> *hospitel*
> *plan air*
> *train*

His cousin Arsenne banged on the door to use the toilet but Flambeau did not even lift his head.

> *polic*
> *ship*
> *aliv e*
> *tran staton*
> *lost*

40

*Morgue* was written on the bottom of the page, away from the others, and it was spelt *M-O-R-G*.

When Flambeau opened the toilet door, a pool of urine and a pile of sodden underwear was waiting in the passage. A gift from Arsenne.

He waited in his bed the following morning for the thrashing that would come when Arsenne told on him. He heard the outrage in his cousin's voice rise and fall with the telling, but no punishment followed. He heard Laetitia sigh, pick up Arsenne's soggy clothes and then wipe the floor with a mop. Flambeau wondered if she had come to care for him just a little bit? He could only hope so because he would need a lot of help to climb even the first rung of his ladder.

The softening of feeling between Laetitia and Flambeau was evident over breakfast, and he was grateful for it. When Knight hooted from the concourse below, Flambeau could see that her goodwill did not extend to the dashing Sapeur.

Flambeau could understand his aunt's jealousy over Knight's appearance, but what he didn't know – what no child would – was what it would mean for her if she was seen to condone Knight and his endeavours.

The precariousness of her situation and Didier's erratic behaviour had already begun to shake her fragile reputation as a God-fearing, upright member of the community. Laetitia knew she needed to see Knight off to ensure she consolidated her place on the side of the good and the true.

The divide between the God-fearing Congolese and the world of the Sapeurs was such that they did not cross one another's doorways. There was not so rigid a divide in the Congo, but here in London even close neighbours would withhold greetings if the other were from the opposite camp.

When Knight hooted for Flambeau that morning, Laetitia saw it as a threat to her good name.

She pulled open the kitchen door, saw the tall Sapeur waiting beside his blue car below, and screamed, '*What are you hooting for?*'

He did not answer.

His silence emboldened her. '*There is nothing for you in my house.*'

Flambeau knew the sound of the horn was his quest calling. He tried to silence his aunt by pulling at her arm but she thwacked him away with the back of her hand. He cried out in frustration, '*He is my friend.*'

'*He's a rubbish.*'

'*He's going to help me.*'

'*Help you do what?*' Flambeau turned to see his uncle in the doorway. The child said nothing and looked away.

Didier gestured for Flambeau to come to him. It made the child churn inside to do his bidding, but then what choice did he have?

Knight's car hooter sounded again. Louder this time. Urgent.

Laetitia closed the door on the sound and muttered, '*Fancy pants.*'

Flambeau shouted, '*He's not a fancy pants. He's a Sapeur. And he's going to help me find my mama.*'

His uncle and aunt exchanged a glance, and Flambeau knew he was lost.

Before he could make a run for it Didier pushed Flambeau into the bedroom and locked the door.

The child ran to the window. He watched Knight glide down the hill in his car.

Knight punched the dashboard in frustration as he turned out of the estate, but that wasn't enough to release him from his anger and his sorrow.

He pulled up at the traffic lights still humming with feeling, flicked the volume on his sound system loud enough for the woman in the car in front of him to jump. Then he cracked his forehead down on the steering wheel. The lights changed twice before he lifted it up again.

Flambeau stood as still as stone in the close confines of that too-small room and he wished, momentarily, that he was dead. The skin on his arms itched; his palms and feet broke into a sweat. He had to get out.

He dragged the chest of drawers across the room inch by silent inch until it was underneath the only window without burglar bars. The window was high and small and it took all his skill to begin to manoeuvre his body through it.

He had to stop often to take short, shallow breaths. He worked quietly. All the while he could hear his uncle and aunt conversing in the kitchen.

He sucked in his stomach and continued to pull himself through the impossibly small gap. It seemed for a moment as if he was stuck. He attempted a final push and then slid out of the window in a rush as if the frame had tasted his desperation and spat him out in distaste.

He bent over double as he passed the kitchen window then tumbled down the stairs.

He flew down them. It felt as if he was falling. His wild young body twisted, turned and kicked off the walls until he spilt out onto the courtyard at the bottom.

Flambeau ran all the way to the minicab office. He smiled when he saw Knight's blue car parked on the yellow line outside.

Knight had a deal with the cabal of Nigerian parking attendants who ran these streets. They were tough, but Knight paid them well for ignoring his illegally parked car and sometimes passed on useful Congo business. He was an African. A brother.

Flambeau couldn't have known this, but it wasn't a good day in the minicab office.

Sometimes it seemed to Eleanor that the clients saved up all their angst and melancholy just for her. 'Yeah? Okay, so it's not a good morning.' She shouted down the phone, 'Aye. I'm sorry she left you, lad, but where do you want to go? Ten minutes. Twelve pounds. Want us? Okay then.'

When Eleanor saw Flambeau in the doorway she got up to meet him.

'Can I talk to Knight?' he said.

Eleanor could see the vein in the child's skinny neck pulsing fast as a hummingbird's wing-beat. She said gently, 'He's got someone with him. You'll have to wait.'

Flambeau started out by sitting on one of the row of orange plastic chairs but it didn't take long for him tire of that. He crawled onto the scratchy nylon carpet, stretched himself out like a green bean, and listened.

The voices coming from Knight's office rose and fell. The roll and cadence of the words in Lingala and Kinyarwanda were spiked now and then with an exclamation, a *ts ts ts* or an *eish*!

They took him home.

Flambeau closed his eyes and rested in the shade of the familiar sounds. He would have loved it less if he had been able to understand what they were saying, but they were too far away for that.

A pair of two-tone shoes caught Flambeau's eye from his vantage point on the green synthetic carpet. Beautiful two-tone shoes with an inch and a half heel.

Flambeau peered out from under the chairs and saw a man dressed in a postman's uniform. He had to be a Sapeur postman. He had to be Congolese. And he was. Voluptuous, glowing brown skin, full mouth, round cheeks and a laugh lurking on the edge of his eyes. Postman even made the uniform of the Royal Mail look good.

'*Bonjour, chérie*. I'm looking for the Knight,' he said to Eleanor.

Eleanor snapped, 'I'm not your *chérie*. And you had the Knight – all night.'

Flambeau hit his head on the red plastic chair as he got up to look. Through his ten-year-old eyes he could see Eleanor was jealous.

'He's got someone with him,' Eleanor said to the Postman.

'I'll wait,' he said.

'Not here you won't,' she snapped.

The Postman laughed at her rudeness and shook his head as if to say it didn't have to be that way but if she insisted on being a bitch he was going to have to pull rank.

'I earned my time with him, sister, way back in the Ndjili slums. Were you there? Because I didn't see you,' he said, and then he cocked his head and waited for her comeback.

Eleanor's voice was tight when she hissed, 'You still have to wait.'

The Postman sighed and sat on the orange plastic chair directly over Flambeau's head.

Now Flambeau could see Postman's shoes up close. He reached out to touch them. The Postman felt the movement around his ankle and looked down to see the boy looking up at him.

Flambeau murmured in Lingala, '*Nice shoes.*'

Postman let out a deep, rumbling laugh, '*You like them?*'

'*Ehe.*'

'*Lacroix.*'

'*Ah.*' Another name to be stored away and pored over later.

'*What's your name, homeboy?*' asked Postman.

'*Flam . . .*'

A sharp sound came from Knight's office which wasn't voice or laughter but it was human – a sort of a gasp – a frightening sound.

The Postman looked up. Flambeau twisted out from under the chairs. Eleanor put down the phone.

'Who's in there with him?' asked the Postman.

Eleanor shrugged. 'Tall man, dark, with a diamond earring.'

'Alone?'

'Two others.'

The Postman was on his feet, '*Merde.*'

They heard a cry, muffled, but absolutely there. Without thinking, Flambeau set off down the passage. Postman grabbed his arm. '*Wait.*'

The door to the office opened. A man loomed in the doorway, the sweat of effort shining on his face, his eyes slightly dilated.

'Deo?' said Postman.

The man regarded Postman, then stepped out and said languorously, '*My friend.*'

Postman's natural ebullience was dulled by dread as he watched Deo walk down the passage towards him. His fingers shook so he tucked them under his arms. It was all he could do to stand his ground.

Deo said, '*It has been too long.*'

'*It has been long,*' murmured the Postman.

The ensuing silence made Eleanor's quivering voice sound all the more shrill. 'And who in the name of the good Lord Jesus are you?'

Deo whipped around, malevolent.

One glance was enough for her. Eleanor reached for the phone.

Deo didn't even look at her as he lashed out with his arm and sent the phone to the floor.

Flambeau began to cry quietly. Deo noticed him for the first time. 'And who is this?'

Postman mumbled, 'Nobody.'

Deo looked at the terrified child and hissed, '*Tais-toi.*'

Flambeau fell silent.

Just then, the door to the minicab office opened with a groan. All eyes flickered in the direction of the sound. A car roared past. A woman pushing a stroller ambled by. But no one entered.

Flambeau whimpered.

Then the doorway filled with the shape of a person. There was something disquieting about how he was moving. It took a moment for Flambeau to realise that it was an old man and that he was entering backwards.

It took the elderly man's complete attention to negotiate his frail passage through the door and around to face forward again.

Flambeau watched him as he found his bearings and then seemed to lose it again. Eleanor and Postman did the same. Even Deo was reduced to observing the old man's uncertain entrance.

The crow-like stoop of his back. The pale, near-foetal transparency of his skin. His bone-and-sinew hand clenched tight around the handle of his shopping trolley. This life, so vividly near its end, made Deo's casual malice seem all the more aberrant.

The old man paid not the slightest attention to Deo and Postman as he passed them by. He stopped in front of Eleanor and said in a voice shaky with age and uncertainty, 'I need to go to my wife.'

Eleanor waited for more and then murmured, 'Where is your wife?'
'At home.'

'Right,' she said.

The old man did not follow with his address even though he could see she was waiting for it. Eleanor realised from his darting, panic-filled eyes that he no longer knew it.

Eleanor offered him her hand. He clutched her fingers gratefully. It was a kind gesture. It moored him to the unreliable earth. The old man took a breath.

Eleanor said gently, 'Where is home?'

He hesitated a moment and then he said, 'Behind the gasworks.' It was clear he could remember nothing more precise than that.

Deo watched Eleanor, wary as a snake.

Eleanor picked up the radio, 'Where are you, sixteen? Anyone near? Come in, nine . . .' She glanced at Flambeau, and he saw a calm in her eyes that reassured him.

'Behind the gasworks,' muttered the old man. 'Been living there for thirty-two years.'

'Take a seat, love. Your driver will be here in five minutes and you can show him the way,' said Eleanor.

Deo swung away, thwarted. He put his arm around Postman's reluctant shoulder and turned to walk out of the room with him in tow. His henchmen clattered out of Knight's office and followed on.

The Postman glanced back at Flambeau and said, '*Watch my boy.*' And then he was gone.

Knight made no sound as he lay prone on the office floor, but Eleanor and Flambeau could see that his eyes followed them as they approached. He lifted his arm and Eleanor saw the gash in his wrist.

'Get a clean dishcloth from under the sink,' she said to Flambeau as she pressed her hand over the wound, 'Get them all.'

Flambeau did as she asked, and together they wrapped the cloths around the wound and stemmed the flow of blood with the pressure of their grip.

'That's better,' she said when the blood no longer seeped through the cloth.

Knight reached across to touch her cheek. She brushed his hand away and said, 'Who are they, Knight?'

Knight sighed.

She asked again, 'Who the bloody hell are they?'

Knight turned to look at Flambeau. 'Tell her, homeboy.'

Flambeau looked at Eleanor. 'They are Congo gangsters.'

She looked down at her young friend. 'That's it? That's all?'

Flambeau shrugged. 'Crooks.'

Knight murmured, 'They've gone now.'

Eleanor sucked air into her lungs very slowly so she could feel the cool air mixing with the tepid. In Scotland, people didn't go to work in their ordinary, everyday offices only to have gangsters nearly slice off their hands. Children were not trafficked halfway across the world. Mothers didn't leave their boys to be raised by unfit relatives for months and months and then not show up when they said they would.

In Scotland, things remained the same. Every morning Eleanor's ma told her she looked like a Highland cow with her hair always so wild about her head. And this when she had just pulled a brush through it a few minutes before, with half a slice of toast in her mouth and a cup of tea in her hand.

For fourteen years she had walked along the same stretch of road to school with her pa, and every last person they passed on each of

those days would say, 'Good day to yer, Eleanor. And to you, Peter.'
And she would nod her head and reply, 'And good day to you.'

Those very people might well have hit their wives behind closed
doors and died a death of loneliness in the long winter months, but
at least they had the decency to be at the same place at the same time
every day and to expect the same of her.

She liked things to be the way they were meant to be.

Knight looked at her and he said, 'They are gone now, *chérie*.'

Flambeau jumped to his feet. 'Can we go too?'

'Where to?' asked Knight.

'To look for mama.'

Eleanor looked at the child as if he must be from a strange and
alien planet. 'Knight's going to the hospital, Flambeau. He needs
stitches,' she said.

Flambeau looked at her. 'And after that? Can we go after that?'

Knight closed his eyes.

'Can we?' The child was desperate. 'Can we?'

That's when Eleanor turned on him and roared, 'What is wrong
with you people?'

She wasn't proud of what she said next, but it burst out of her
mouth like bile as she got to her feet. 'Get out of here, Flambeau.
Just . . . go!'

# Au Revoir, Merci

The way Flambeau flew along the pavement had an ungainly, precarious speed to it, as if he were pursued by a terrible foe. He flashed past a slight black woman with large sunglasses as she carefully carried her shopping home. She turned in alarm to see what horror drove him onward.

The boy was racing just ahead of his breaking heart.

The blue light denoting the Tottenham Police Station shone from across the street. Flambeau saw the word *police* . . . he stopped to read it, heart thumping, breath bursting, *police*. He pulled a folded piece of paper out of his pocket and he found the word halfway up his list . . . *polic*.

At least he had this: thanks to his ma, he had his Jacob's ladder.

He stood there for a moment considering the other options on the page, then he folded the paper carefully and put it back in his pocket. He took a deep breath and crossed the road.

The counter in the police station was higher than Flambeau's head. All Flambeau could see, now that he was pressed up against the counter, was the policeman's eyes and forehead. Pale eyes, freckles and a ginger fringe above. 'What did you say your mother's name was?'

'She was supposed to be here yesterday,' said Flambeau quietly.

'Answer my question,' said the policeman.

Flambeau looked at the policeman and didn't know what to say.

'What is her name?' the officer asked again.

'Bijou.' Flambeau whispered it in the hope that it would not be heard.

'What'd you say, boy?'

Flambeau looked up and said, 'I don't know . . . I don't know what name she had on the plane.'

And the thing is, he wasn't lying. That's how it looked, but it wasn't how it was. The officer stopped writing and looked at Flambeau.

'How many has she got?' asked the officer.

Somebody laughed in the charge office beyond. It was frightening laughter, but Flambeau couldn't see who it came from.

The officer waited. The boy shuffled and then tried again. 'The man in the hat gave me a new name when he put me on the plane.'

'What man is that?' asked the policeman.

Flambeau knew then that it was all over. The policeman had a slick line of moisture building on his upper lip. Flambeau couldn't take his eyes off it. He could hear a quickening in the policeman's words when he spoke. 'And what is your name when you are not on the plane?'

The flap door into the charge office opened and Flambeau saw the policeman beyond, pricked-eared.

Flambeau spoke in his most polite voice. The one his mother told him to use for priests and soldiers. Maybe it would have worked if he'd said it in French, but in English it came out wrong, 'You be the best, sir, God, and I thank you very much. *Au revoir. Merci.*'

Flambeau clapped his hands in that African way to show great respect. He bent his head down and clapped his way to the back wall and there he froze. The policeman turned away from him and made the smallest of gestures.

Afterwards, Flambeau wasn't sure whether it had even happened. All he knew was that all of a sudden there were two policemen in front of him. One of them leaned down into his face and said, 'Your address, son. Right. Bloody. Now.'

Even from way down in the courtyard Flambeau could see the shock in Didier's body at the sight of the two policemen in his doorway.

If Didier was afraid, then Flambeau had good reason to be too. The only thing he couldn't decide was whom to fear most, the policemen or his uncle.

He was dry-mouthed as he followed the red-haired policeman up the stairs. It felt like a long way.

By the time he got to the door, Didier was spelling out his name, '. . . i . . . s . . . i . . . n . . . g . . . o.

'Mr M-as-is-in-go . . .' The fat policeman pronounced the name horribly, but Didier laughed anyway, servile as a puppy. The policeman asked, 'The boy says his mother was supposed to arrive in London yesterday?'

Didier wrung his hands, but said nothing. Flambeau looked at his uncle and it dawned on him that he didn't understand a word of English.

The man was such a power in the household that it had never occurred to Flambeau that he wasn't like that in the world. But there he was, unable even to understand a simple question and willing to do anything to please these people who could scupper his application for amnesty. It made him limp and vicious.

It did cross the child's mind that now would be a good time to abandon his uncle in retribution for all his wrongs, but instead he mumbled a translation of the policeman's question. '*He's asking why my mother didn't come.*'

Didier looked at the fat policeman and laughed. '*Ah, monsieur l'officier . . . ce n'est pas la vérité.*'

And that's what he got for his trouble. Lies. Flambeau was not going to translate that even though they all expected it.

Didier stepped in with more. '*C'est tout imaginé, monsieur le sergeant.*'

The fat policeman considered Didier's grey face. 'You saying that none of what this child is saying is true?'

Flambeau waited. Not even his uncle would dare to claim that. The boy bit his lip.

Then Didier nodded his head.

Jesus! Flambeau felt a small tidal wave of nausea rising.

The fat policeman looked from the boy to Didier and asked, 'You his family?'

Didier nodded his head.

The other policeman opened the door behind Didier with his foot and so revealed the three grim and silent men in the passage behind it.

Pastor Gold Tooth was one of them. Flambeau could see that he was decked in too much beauty and too much gold to look to these policemen like a man of the cloth.

'And them? Are they family too?' asked the officer.

Didier said nothing. The policeman looked to Flambeau for help, so the child was forced to translate once more. '*The white man wants to know who they are.*'

'*They are my Church Council, sir,*' said Didier. Flambeau mumbled, 'My uncle says they . . .'

But Didier hissed, '*Call him sir. I said sir.*' Flambeau began again. 'Sir. He says they are his Church Council. Sir.'

The thin policeman turned away, 'Right. And I'm Postman fucking Pat.'

# Laetitia

One of the places Laetitia loved most in the world was the laundromat across from the station in White Hart Lane. She often sat there, leaning back against the plastic chair with her head between two washing machines as they swished their contents to and fro. She remained long after her washing was clean and dry. There, she was blessedly free of the mess of human need that surrounded her at home. It gave her respite.

Today she found it less restful. Every time she closed her eyes the fact of Flambeau locked in the room at home with his longing and disappointment took occupation of her, woke her, roused her. *Merde!*

She would never have admitted it, but part of her feared what her husband might do when left alone with the child. She was not blind to Didier's increasingly volatile exchanges with Flambeau, but she had no idea what to do about it. Getting help was the province of the entitled. *There's a coffin waiting for you in Bukavu, Laetitia, you and your children.*

So she just put one foot in front of the other and hoped that God might step in and show Didier the way back to reason.

Laetitia stood up with a sigh, folded her laundry neatly and walked back to the flat.

She called out as she opened the front door but there was no response. The air sat heavy and still around her body. She called again. Perhaps the child had escaped into sleep? Didier's absence was a greater mystery; she could only hope, again, that he was buying bread, or perhaps milk, in the local shop.

She reheated the pondu from the night before and opened the bedroom door to wake Flambeau with a bowl of food.

Laetitia stood in the doorway of the empty room and waited for the familiar rush of rage to fill her at what she saw as Flambeau's insolence, but it didn't come. A much darker feeling settled on her, a fear, a deep, quiet feeling that he may be gone forever.

She ran up to the roof. A broken catty lay on the ground, the only clue to Flambeau's prior presence there.

She had her wits about her enough to change from her threadbare tracksuit into decent clothes before she ran down to the school. She looked through the fence at the children playing.

Flambeau was not in the playground. Laetitia knew he wouldn't be. She was only at that fence because she didn't know where else to look.

She heard a voice and looked up. His teacher, Miss Glenys, was smiling through the fence at her, mildly suspicious, 'Can I help you?'

Laetitia looked at the young woman's plump, white face. She would have liked to have said, '*Yes, please. Help me find my sister's child. Calm my husband. Grant me political asylum. Make me beautiful again.*'

But Laetitia knew what would follow. '*Oh, so YOU are Flambeau's aunt. I have waited for you at all three parent–teacher meetings. Social services are planning a visit. Such a bright boy, Flambeau.*'

It filled Laetitia with shame that this woman would know her failings, so she simply stepped back and said, '*Non merci, madame.* And thank you.'

Knight's blue car was parked outside the minicab office with its hazard lights flashing. Laetitia found herself running towards it, certain that it contained Flambeau and that he was hurt.

The pain evident in Knight's face as he sat in the passenger seat surprised her. His arm was bandaged and he groaned as Eleanor popped the clutch and the car leapt forward. 'Slowly, *chérie*,' he admonished her.

Laetitia knocked on the window. He glanced up at the older woman and then reluctantly rolled down the window to hear what she had to say.

Laetitia could only manage, '*You are hurt.*'

He simply looked at her.

Eleanor took pity on Laetitia sufficiently to lean forward from the driver's seat and say, 'Don't stand too close to this car. I can't be trusted.'

Laetitia stepped back onto the pavement. Knight looked at her more carefully now. He could see that the shrew of this morning had been chastened. Eleanor ground the wheel rim against the pavement and Knight grimaced at Laetitia. '*She learnt to drive in a fishing boat.*'

Laetitia sucked in her breath and said, '*I'm looking for the boy.*'

Knight shook his head. '*Haven't seen him.*'

Laetitia looked away. '*Help me. Please.*'

Knight could see her fear. He knew what her thumping, red heart would look like if he held it in his hand. He turned his head towards her and said, '*He went to find his mother.*'

Laetitia nodded her head. In her mind's eye she could see Bijou turn on her with her eyes-like-coals and say, '*You lost my boy. My only child.*'

Laetitia hated her sister.

Bijou came out of their mother's womb with the power to bend the world to her will. When she danced with her friends in the schoolyard she was a siren sent by the God of mischief to drive the boys mad.

Whereas Laetitia was always filled with a heaviness of body and spirit that was more often true of the last-born, when the riches of the mother's body had been used up.

Laetitia married early to get away, and for a time she and Didier had the beginnings of a dignified life. But everyone knows that war has no truck with dignity, and when the bloodthirsty Hutu Genocidaire flowed over the border from Rwanda to slaughter the Banyamulenge, it was to Bijou's house that she and Didier were forced to flee. And it was Bijou's thoughtful, civil servant husband who paid for Laetitia and Didier to flee to safety. First to Uganda and then, five years later, to London.

And this is what Laetitia had done in return. She had lost her sister's one and only child.

The bright-blue car jumped forward once more. Knight hit the dashboard in frustration. Eleanor shouted, 'Sorry, okay. I'm doing my best. Jesus!'

Knight pushed open the door and said, '*Merde!* Just park it here. Turn it off and leave it here.'

'Right here?' she asked.

Knight slammed the door, 'Get out before you crash my car.' He waited for Eleanor to turn off the engine and then he turned to look at Laetitia. He would have liked to have comforted her but he just said, '*If he comes, I will tell him you were here.*'

It was the best he could do. Then he walked into the minicab office.

Laetitia turned slowly and walked away. Eleanor struggled out of the car, pink with stress and exertion. She saw Laetitia start her slow walk up the hill. She wanted to call to her, to ask her to tell Flambeau she was sorry for sending him away. But the curve of Laetitia's back did not lend itself to being a message-bearer.

Flambeau typically scuttled under things when he was afraid. That's what he did when he ran away from the police that day. He hid in the sheets, saris and towels that dried on the washing line. He crawled into their cover until he felt like an ant under the earth.

When his heart had stopped pounding sufficiently for him to take a deep breath, Flambeau climbed onto an apple box and stuck his head out above the laundry.

Didier's blue front door, three floors up, looked deserted. The stairway too. And the fire escape. Then Flambeau saw his uncle.

Didier was pacing at the far edge of the balcony. He moved in a jerky, agitated way. He scanned the courtyard beyond him. The child didn't have to think too hard to know who he was looking for.

Flambeau ducked back in between the sanctuary of the sheets but he knew they wouldn't keep him safe forever.

When he saw Laetitia drag herself across the courtyard with a shopping bag some hours later, he was still too scared to emerge and hungrier than a horse.

The sight of Flambeau gesturing to her from the washing line made Laetitia stop in her tracks and weep silently with relief. She stood there for a moment, rocking on her heels.

The quiet centre of the clean, sweet-smelling laundry was comforting and mysteriously peaceful. Laetitia sat on the apple crate and breathed a sigh.

A pair of ragged floral sheets hung before and behind her like the bread in a sandwich.

She touched Flambeau's cheek. He glanced at her in surprise. She found herself thinking that she was truly glad that this boy, who had his mother's eyes and her dazzling smile, had come back.

Who would have thought it.

Flambeau longed to lean against his aunt and take comfort, but he knew not to test this brief kindness.

He didn't want to tell her about the visit from the police. He didn't want to feel her panic and her wrath. Instead, he said the thing that was truer than all of that. 'I want to go to where Mama is.'

It was spoken with such longing that Laetitia had to dig in her shopping bag in order to stop him seeing her eyes well up.

She pulled out a loaf of bread. Tore off a chunk and gave it to him. He took it.

Flambeau spoke quietly. '*I didn't mean for them to come here, Aunt.*' Laetitia looked up in a snap. '*Who?*'

Flambeau was too afraid to look at her when he said, '*The police.*' He put his head in his hands. '*I went to ask for help. I needed help.*'

Just when he thought she was going to poke out his eyes, she grabbed him and held him close. Then his aunt struggled to her feet. '*Wait until dark.*'

He held onto her arm. She brushed him off. '*When he sleeps. Don't come back until he sleeps.*'

Flambeau watched his aunt weave her way through the sheets towards the stairs, ragged tired.

He ate his bread. Then he turned the apple box on its side and folded himself up inside it.

It was dark night when Flambeau lifted the post flap and hissed his cousin's name into it. 'Elvira.' There was no response. He hissed again, this time a little louder. Then there were footsteps and the door opened.

His cousin didn't offer him any greeting when he passed into the hallway but he had long ago stopped expecting such kindness. She said something else that made his heart stop for a moment. '*It's your fault. All your fault.*'

She brushed past him and went into the bedroom. He heard the sound of the snick-snick of a young child crying in its sleep but he didn't move towards it.

His eyes adjusted to the dark. He saw a shape sitting in the armchair in the living room. He moved closer.

The shock of his aunt sitting there clad only in a petticoat halted his passage. Voluptuous breasts and thick upper arms sagged vulnerable, open, bare. She heard him but did not turn her face towards him.

He crept forward.

She coughed a wheezy cough. Lifted a blood-sodden tissue away from her lip.

He could see now that her whole face was swollen. He touched her shoulder.

A gust of movement brought her head between her knees. She vomited onto the floor.

He turned and he ran.

The clouds raced across the sky very fast. Flambeau lay on the mesh roof of the birdhouse as if suspended in space. A brown cloud of birds swept by underneath him.

Sally uncoiled herself slowly in response, her skin rustling slightly as she moved.

Flambeau flipped over to see her coming. She was beautiful and animated as she slithered like a ripple across the floor. He whispered, '*Hello, Sally.*' And then he closed his eyes.

# Snake Boy

Flambeau was so still as he sat on the floor of the children's bedroom that he seemed not to be breathing. He was waiting for something but you could tell by looking at him that he had no real hope that it would happen.

Morning sunshine blasted through the window, hot and humid already. All the beds were neatly made.

When he heard the scream, it was as if Christmas morning had come. *Thank you!* Flambeau smiled. Then he covered himself with a blanket.

Didier stood in front of his cupboard howling like a hyena. In the drawer before him was Sally the snake, curled up in his boxer shorts.

Three frightened children crowded together in the doorway.

Laetitia could hardly open her eyes to take in the cause of the chaos.

Flambeau knew, even before they got there, that they were going to see Pastor Gold Tooth. His feet hardly touched the ground as his uncle marched him along the pavement. Laetitia followed, bent over from her injuries.

Flambeau prayed under his ten-year-old breath that Gold Tooth would not flay him for his sin with the snake.

The Pastor took his time looking over Laetitia's bruises. Long enough for Flambeau to dare to hope that his uncle would get the flak and not himself.

Gold Tooth turned away from Laetitia and sat in a faded armchair under a glowing portrait of himself. He made no sound apart from a deep '*Tsk. Tsk. Tsk*' in the back of his throat. Didier's foot began to gyrate up and down.

Mrs Gold Tooth was a beauty. Today she wore a silver T-shirt which moved in soft waves as she poured a cup of tea and handed it to Laetitia. She made no move to offer any to Didier or the Pastor. That was her way of showing solidarity with Laetitia. Then she got up to leave.

No one likes to get beaten. Not children. Not women. No one. It doesn't stop it happening to deny someone a cup of tea but at least it shows that you see it and that you mind.

The Pastor scowled at Mrs Gold Tooth's retreating back and then poured tea for himself and Didier. He handed him the cup and asked, '*What about the boy's mother?*'

It seemed to Flambeau that the adults in the room drew together at his question. Without even moving they made a coven of grown-up bodies that rendered him invisible.

Didier murmured, '*We know she left Kinshasa and that she landed in London.*'

What? Flambeau jolted upright. She what? It was only his survival skills which kept him from shouting out, '*Where? Where is she?*'

He knew if he broke the spell of their collusion he would be cast out. So he made himself listen, heart thumping in his chest.

Didier said, '*If she is in London she'll go to Le Pitch.*'

Laetitia scoffed. '*Broadwater Farm? Rubbish. She'll come for the child before she goes dancing.*'

Flambeau leant in still further. He made a mental note to himself to add *Le Pitch* to his Jacob's ladder even though he had no idea where it was.

Didier snarled at his wife. '*Pah. She would dance before anything else. She would dance even if it was on my grave, that one.*'

Laetitia spat at his slander. '*And you would follow her around the dance floor like a puppy. Watching her hips and her legs with spit drooling off your chin. Remember how you did that?*'

That's when Didier shouted, '*This is London.*'

'*And so?*'

'*And so you are a fool if you don't know that the Devil lives here . . .*'

They all stopped, unsettled by the feeling in his face.

Laetitia sat back in her chair. It was vividly clear to her, just then, that Didier had taken his final step out of the rational world. That his Devil was not the same as hers. That sometime between Flambeau running away and the feel of Didier's fist on her face, she had lost him to his madness.

She could tell that the Pastor saw it too.

Didier misunderstood their pause as agreement and continued, '*Le Pitch. You can find the Devil there . . . along with all the Kinshasa gangsters. And your sister.*'

Laetitia looked at him. The man was humming with paranoia. His fist hit his palm, thwack, his fingers closed around it and he muttered, '*God has turned his back on Broadwater Farm.*'

She would have liked to laugh at him but her face hurt too much; instead she spat out her disdain. '*Gah!*'

Didier lashed out quick as a snake. It was only the Pastor's sudden hiss that stopped him from hitting her.

Flambeau forgot that he was invisible. He stepped forward to protect her and he kicked Gold Tooth's chair instead. He froze.

The Pastor turned on him, as if seeing him for the first time. They looked at one another then the pastor spoke very quietly. '*Snake boy.*'

It was so malevolent a sound that Flambeau looked away. Then stepped back.

The Pastor didn't take his eyes off the boy, not for one second. The silence in the room was terrible.

Flambeau summoned his courage from the deepest well and still he shook with fear when he returned the pastor's gaze and asked, '*Where is this place?*'

All three adult faces turned to him.

'*This place you call Le Pitch?*'

What happened next was just a quick exchange of looks between the men but it was enough for Flambeau to know they were never going to tell him.

He knocked a red glass ashtray onto the floor on his way to the door.

He was a small and chaotic thing as he raced across the black tar of the desolate housing estate. It did not take long for Didier to overtake him.

Flambeau struggled to pull away from his uncle's grasp. He kicked and hit and cried out; it was searing.

Gold Tooth advanced across the courtyard with a measured pace. He made up for his lack of speed with a crack to Flambeau's face that sent the boy to the ground.

The two women watched from the balcony as Gold Tooth barked at the child to stand up.

Flambeau tried to move, but he was unable to tell his legs and arms what to do. Again the Pastor commanded, '*Get up.*'

This time it sounded like death coming. It was adrenalin that got Flambeau to his feet. He bowed his head low on his thumping, defeated chest.

'*Your mother's fate is in God's hands.*' Gold Tooth hissed, very close to Flambeau's ear. '*And you, boy? Do you know God?*'

The God Flambeau knew was a loving God but in church that evening amongst his people Flambeau wondered if God had turned against him too.

Word of Flambeau's infraction seemed to have spread like pollen on the wind and once-friendly faces now regarded him with hooded eyes. *The child put a serpent in his uncle's underwear. A serpent!*

The village had cast him out.

The only one amongst them who seemed unsure of this course was Laetitia. She took her usual place at the drum machine and then turned and caught his eye. She smiled at him, infinitely sad.

Pastor Gold Tooth walked slowly up the aisle towards Flambeau. The child watched his approach and thought he was like a ship, slow and grand and all-knowing. His words boomed. '*And God called all the children to him. And he said unto them . . .*' the Pastor raised his hands above Flambeau's head and blocked out the whole world with his arms, '*. . . we will cast out the Devil.*'

Who? Flambeau's instinct for danger shrieked thumping loud in his ears. He tried to get up. He felt the weight of his uncle's hands on his shoulders.

The Pastor was close enough to drop a bead of sweat from his brow onto the boy's cheek. '*He will have no purchase amongst us.*'

A hundred arms swayed in a roof of moving branches above Flambeau's head. Loud, ecstatic prayer rose in amongst the moving limbs, calling out to be seen and heard.

Flambeau felt his cousin Elvira slip off the pew beside him. She hit the floor at his feet. Laetitia cried out. He caught a glimpse of his aunt at the drum machine, anxious, fearful.

Elvira jerked and foamed at the mouth on the floor. The surrounding women got to their knees to give her succour. They lifted her and carried her comatose from the room.

Flambeau was afraid. As he looked around the room the people seem to be asking the same of him. They spoke in the shrill voice of the righteous. *If you want to remain amongst us, you must submit.* Their voices rose fever-pitch high.

He had to get up. Hands pressed him down. He fought back. He would not fall or foam at the mouth.

The Pastor sensed his rebellion, and he would have none of it. He loomed close and then closer still. Flambeau stood up and the big man crashed him to the ground face first. His mouth tasted dust. Hands pinned him down.

Right then, in the midst of all that noise and terror Flambeau heard a sound, distant but entirely distinct. *Kaaakakaka.* And again, *Kaaakakaka.*

It could have been the feet stamping or maybe the sound of the hand-clapping bouncing off the window and coming back ten-fold, or maybe it was the memory of his mama – whatever it was, it gave him the strength to twist himself away from them all. He tore his desperate head free of their hands, stood up and roared.

They could not have him because he belonged to someone else.

# Horns and Tails

Feathers floated in the sky in deep and perfect silence.

They landed on Flambeau's grave face like snow. He closed his eyes. He did not move a muscle until he was almost completely covered.

Eleanor thought he was dead when she saw him there on the rooftop with a mask of white over his face. He didn't move when she said his name.

She went right up close to hear if he was still breathing and that's when his eyes flicked open and her heart nearly stopped. 'Shit!' she said and stepped back. Then she asked, 'Are you sick?'

He looked up at her. Whatever he was, it was not pretty.

'Sorry I had a go at you yesterday,' she murmured. 'I was scared.'

Flambeau shrugged. Then he leant forward to ask, 'Knight okay?'

'Oh, he'll be fine. Got some stitches.'

Then Eleanor saw Eugene. He was sweeping a pile of feathers into the corner of the birdcage as if nothing was amiss. As if there wasn't a distraught boy beside him with a mask of death over his eyes.

Eugene turned and worked his way back towards them. Flambeau lifted his feet to make way for the man and his broom. Eugene muttered, 'I don't mind cleaning up when it's me that makes the mess . . .'

Eleanor snapped, 'It's a wonder you make it to the end of the day with all you have to do, Eugene.'

That shut him up. He was not happy but he was silent apart from his broom swishing, and that was a blessing.

Eugene had a thing for Eleanor. From the first time he saw her, he had wanted to kiss her swollen red mouth. She was too long-faced for conventional prettiness, but when the light was right the angles of her face revealed a rare beauty.

Loving her reminded him that he had nothing to do with his life except listen to heavy metal, eat bacon and eggs and be the Saint Francis of Assisi of the East End.

Flambeau picked a feather out of his mouth. He looked up at Eleanor and said, 'Do you know this place Bradwutefarm?'

'Who?'

'Bradwatefarm. Bruddwatre Farm?'

Eleanor told him it sounded like a German sausage, but he didn't laugh.

Flambeau looked at her and said, 'Can I sleep at you tonight?'

'What?' she asked, alarmed by the request. In Scotland a neighbour of twenty years might ask for a bed if his roof blew off in a storm, but not before that passage of time and not without profound need.

And then there was his aunt. Eleanor told Flambeau that the ferocious Laetitia would chop her head off if she let him stay with her. She told him that so he would laugh and go home to his family, but he didn't.

The child was so still that he reminded her of the hunter he had been on the first day she ever saw him. Except now his stillness was darker than anything she'd seen before apart from her dad's dead face.

All she could think to say was, 'I was going to dye my hair.'

The boy didn't look up at her, but Eugene did. 'Why would you do that?'

Flambeau spoke very quietly. 'Because Knight likes blondes.'

Her glance was sharp. 'How do you know that?' she snapped.

'He is a Sapeur,' said Flambeau, as if it was the most obvious thing in the world.

He wanted a blonde. It was true. But she didn't want Flambeau to say it like that. To say it for her. It made her feel the chalk of shame in her mouth. She turned her back on the boy. 'Bloody hell, Flambeau.'

He watched her, bewildered and then horrified. He had no idea what he had said to offend her.

Eleanor felt a throbbing in her head and sweat building behind her ears. It seemed to her just then that Flambeau was a savant of the human heart and that hers was in no shape for observation.

'Bloody hell,' she said again, and then she walked away across the shining rooftop.

'Wait!' said Flambeau, but she did not respond. She pulled open the door and then she was gone.

Flambeau shuddered. He stared at the door, willing her to come back.

But she did not.

'It's Broadwater Farm you are looking for, mate,' said Eugene with an air of superiority.

Flambeau stood up so fast he hit his head on a beam. 'You know where it is?'

'Adams Road.'

'Will you show me?'

'It's the arse end of the world and I'll be the only white face in it,' said Eugene.

Flambeau didn't know what to say to that.

Eugene did though. 'Tell the truth, I don't know why you lot keep coming here. Like rats to a stinking ship.'

'Tomorrow? Will you show me it tomorrow?' asked the boy.

'I'm off to Manchester tomorrow.'

'When will you be back?' said Flambeau, his heart thumping loud in his chest.

'My sister is going to take Sally,' said Eugene. 'Will you feed the birds?'

'Two days? One day?' asked the boy.

'It's not for me. This stinking ship of a place.'

And that was that.

Flambeau looked at Eugene, hardly daring to ask, and then he said, 'I need a place to sleep tonight.'

Flambeau's words hung in the air for a moment.

They brought discomfort and unease to Eugene's pale face.

'You want to sleep at my place?' he asked.

Flambeau nodded his head.

Eugene considered the boy and then he shrugged. 'I don't barely know you, mate. I don't know you one bit.'

Flambeau looked at him and then he said, 'I have nowhere to go.'

It was a statement of fact, unsentimental and irrefutable.

Eugene rested the broom against his widening girth and sighed.

The swifts in the cage swept from one side to another in a swarm. Flambeau waited for Eugene's word.

The sun went behind a cloud.

Eugene finally shook his head. 'Can't take that kind of risk, can ya? I mean, you aren't family or anything.' He started sweeping again. 'Just can't be sure.'

Thank God Eleanor opened the door when she did because who knows what Flambeau would have done next.

She saw him there with his eyes like saucers and she said, very softly, *she remembers how softly it was*, she said, 'Come on then.'

Flambeau ate his way through three tins of baked beans before she could even heat them up. He wiped his mouth on a dishcloth, washed his bowl out and said he was ready to help Eleanor dye her hair.

He sat on the cistern, feet on the closed loo bowl, with the timer in his hand. There was something heartbreaking in his seriousness, as if he was sure she would throw him out if he didn't do a good job.

The bleach she put on her hair stung after a few seconds. Then it began to burn. She was desperate. 'Talk to me, Flambeau. Sing. Tell me a joke.'

But it wasn't a joke-telling kind of day, and for all his eagerness to please he just wasn't able to entertain her. 'Sorry.'

'S'okay,' she said.

They sat in silence. Then Flambeau spoke. 'Eugene said it was Broadwater Farm.'

'What?'

'That place, the one with the dancing . . . remember? It's in Adams Road.'

'Yeah,' she said, 'I've heard of Adams Road. Round here some-where.'

She looked at him and he at her. She knew he wanted more, but she closed her eyes then because the fumes were making her weep. 'Oh God, I'm going blind.'

She hoped he would back off but when she opened her eyes again he was still there, waiting.

She sighed. 'We'll ask one of the drivers to show us tomorrow. Okay?'

Tomorrow would never be soon enough for Flambeau. She knew that. But it would have to do for now.

The boy counted out the seconds as they passed. 'Twenty-six, twenty-five, twenty-four . . .' he looked down at his stopwatch, 'twenty-three, twenty-two . . .'

Eleanor bounced on the balls of her feet to ameliorate the burning of the bleach. 'You know, I didn't give a fig what I looked like until I met Knight the Adonis.' She stopped to take a deep breath. 'It's an almighty drag this beauty business. Please God being a Blondie will make me less of a dishrag,' she muttered, more to herself than to him.

'You're not a dishrag,' said Flambeau.

Maybe not, but Eleanor knew that she was not the one who turned heads as they walked along the street. Had she been Congolese she might have been able to dress in equal sartorial splendour but she was a teacher's daughter from rural Scotland and up there clothes were to keep you warm, or dry, or at the very least, alive. She knew that wasn't enough for Knight.

Eleanor had had an ordinary boyfriend once. He was a fisherman in Kinlochbervie. His name was Gerry MacLean and he really wanted her friend, Gina.

Once, when they'd had a pint too many, he declared undying love for her and talked her into having sex with him on the dunes below the hotel.

Eleanor didn't think Knight and Gerry MacLean were the same species. Because when Knight took her to bed, it didn't feel like the same act. Not even vaguely.

'Gerry MacLean would never have bought me those useless whatsa-ma-callit shoes now, would he?' she said to Flambeau, after she had filled him in.

Flambeau looked at her. 'He would have bought you a fish.'

True. The way he said it made no comment on whether one gift was better than the other. They both had their uses after all.

Flambeau leaned forward to stop a dribble of hair dye making its way into her eye. It made her want to hug him.

The timer sounded. The final countdown had begun. Flambeau called it out. 'Five, four, three, two . . . thirty minutes.'

'Thank you, Jesus!' shrieked Eleanor. She bent over the bath and Flambeau, entranced by the alchemy of her dark locks turning a golden blonde, rinsed off the dye with the showerpiece.

It was a short-lived pleasure.

When she looked at herself in the mirror all she could think to say was, 'I'm still Eleanor the schoolteacher's daughter, no matter what bloody colour my hair is.'

He liked that. 'You're a schoolteacher's daughter,' he said, grinning.

'I was. He's dead now, my dad.'

She could see Flambeau felt the gravity of it for her.

She reached for a towel. Flambeau watched her wind it around her hair.

He tried the same with his own and produced a turban. They were two turbaned heads side by side in the mirror. Then he said, 'My papa was broken up by a grenade. Into pieces.'

She turned to look at him, 'What'd you say?'

She could see him remembering.

'It was more than one.'

She took the towel off her head and watched him tip his from left to right and right to left to see how long it would stay up there, and then he carried on, 'It was a box of them. On the green grass by our house in Bukavu.'

The towel plopped off his head onto the floor. He picked it up. 'The soldiers shot into the box.' he folded the towel meticulously. 'I found his foot. Me and Mama. We buried it.' Then Flambeau handed her the towel, bowed slightly to thank her for it. 'We buried him near his father. And his father's father.' Then he took the towel back and wiped his face.

He turned and looked her straight in the eyes. His own pools were black as pitch as he said, 'They had horns. The soldiers who did it had horns.'

And he marked the side of his temples with his hands. 'Just there. Where their ears should be.'

# Ordinary Men

Flambeau slept on the rickety sofa that night. Wrapped up so entirely in blankets that he looked like a sausage roll.

Eleanor tried Knight's mobile by hitting redial on her keypad until her finger throbbed, and then she tried her ma. She was hoping for a bit of grace. It felt like she was due.

It was her mother's new beau who answered the phone. She told him she was sorry to phone so late. That she couldn't sleep and that she just needed to hear her ma's voice. She told him all that. But he put the phone down without saying a single word and all the bad times came back with a roar.

The worst was when her mother tried to dry her father out – as if he were a herring. She tied him to the bed so he wouldn't make it to the off-licence.

When Eleanor wept and pulled out her hair at his imprisonment, her mother said it would be for just a few days and then his body could begin to get through withdrawal and set about healing itself.

Those nights Eleanor lay in bed and listened to him call her name, 'Eleanor.' Or, ''Nor, darling.' Not once, but on and on and on. He never called for her ma.

At first his calls were sweet but eventually his voice filled with despair and then she knew the abuse was coming.

*She was an ungrateful little bitch just like her ma and why the fuck did he bother to give her all that loving.*

Oh, the way he sounded when he said that would drive her under her pillow or out of her window and onto the roof to get away.

Eleanor understood that it wasn't him talking. She knew that if your body suddenly didn't have what it craved you got the shakes; you shat and pissed when you didn't mean to and you had powerful all-consuming hallucinations.

One time her father saw her burning in flames and he couldn't get free to rescue her. His cries were wild with horror.

Only she wasn't burning in flames, and if she had been, he wouldn't have been able to see her for his visions, let alone save her.

She stood in the passage of her childhood house and wept silently at that fact.

And now she sat in the straight-backed chair in the corner of the living room and watched Flambeau sleep.

She didn't even turn when she heard Knight's key in the lock. By then she was breathing in rhythm with the child's breath.

Knight stood in the quiet half-dark looking at them both.

'He's only here for one night,' she said, in case he thought the child was to stay.

Knight took off his jacket, crossed over to kiss the top of her head and turned on the light. That's when he saw the blonde. 'Aaah. Who is this beauty in my living room?'

'The lad sucked up three tins of baked beans before I even heated them up,' she said. 'And by the way, it's MY living room.'

She said that because she was afraid. She was afraid of what Flambeau had said to her and what it meant for his life. And she was afraid she couldn't pay the rent.

It was the more banal fear that was the less complicated, so it was first to burst out of her mouth. She told Knight he had to bring in some money. The rent was due and she didn't have enough coming in to cover it. Unlike Laetitia's subsidised flat, Eleanor's was privately owned and her landlord punctilious. They had until Friday.

'It's always feast or famine with you,' she said.

'Tomorrow okay, *chérie*?' Knight smiled at her as he said it.

From the twitch she felt inside her stomach she knew there would be nothing from him by Friday.

She was on her own. It made her hungry, 'Want a boiled egg?' she asked.

He shot her with his look, a piercing sort of glance that happened sometimes between them. It felt dangerous to her. He didn't want a boiled egg.

She watched the egg thumping around in the boiling water and he came and stood in the doorway to watch her.

She spoke quietly. 'Flambeau says his father was blown up by the army.'

Knight went very still, then he asked quietly, 'The Presidential Guard or the Génocidaire?'

'I don't know.'

She turned to look at him. 'Why'd they do that?'

'Terror,' and he lifted his head. 'It's called terror.'

She could see that he was tired. Deeply tired. She could have wept for him, but instead she said, 'There's toast?'

He shook his head. 'I want a pondu. Congolese pondu with salt fish and manioc and fufu.' He said it too quietly.

She looked at him.

He wanted the taste of his place so badly, and all she could say was, 'I can do rye, sesame or a bagel.'

She could see it made him want to cry. Right then in the kitchen, she knew that the only way for her to show him that there was life beyond Congolese pondu, salt fish, and all the rest, was to kiss him. So she did.

She kissed his neck, then his nipples, then his belly button. She could feel him coming alive. He snagged her bottom in his hands and lifted her up.

That's when the telephone rang.

If it had been any other time she wouldn't have even heard it but it might've been her ma phoning back. You never give up hope for a bit of grace from your ma.

So she took her hand out of his trousers.

The phone stopped ringing before she got to it and she said, 'Shit. Bet that was my ma.'

He said, 'Then phone her back.'

'Jim might pick up. He's already hung up on me once today.'

Knight knew how Jim had moved in with her ma before her dad was even cold in the ground.

Eleanor turned to Knight and said, 'She must have told him to do that. Bitch!'

Knight looked at her with those grave eyes he got when he disapproved of something she did. He shook his head. 'In Africa we do not talk about our mothers that way.'

'What do you know?' she shouted, close to tears.

He was stung and she should have stopped there, but she didn't; maybe she was just too young and too frightened, 'What do you know about mothers and fathers?' she spat.

She said this to the orphan from the Ndjili slums. Cruel as a weasel.

And wrong. She was dead wrong. He knew his ma in the same way Flambeau knew Bijou. She was his everything.

As far as Knight knew, his mother was one of the first people to die of AIDS in the slum, but no one knew to call it that then.

She was the night cashier at the petrol station when she was infected. Her boss came by every night to collect the takings from the till and one night he lingered awhile.

He didn't need to tell her what he was there for. She could smell it on his skin. She had learnt that odour indecently young. She recognised it.

Knight was a baby under the counter on his blanket at the time. What could she do? What could she say?

The illness colonised her rapidly, her symptoms exacerbated by their poverty.

His mother held on to life until she was thin as a stick . . . just so she could be with her boy.

She used to clap her hands together when she saw him and so communicate her joy, the faint joy of skin and bone touching, so faint, but he knew what she meant.

She couldn't take food or water except when he fed her. Slowly, spoon by spoon, so as not to spill. She made her body keep that food, so that she could look at his face while he fed her.

And then, one day, she couldn't even do that. And she slipped away like a wisp.

Knight looked at Eleanor. She knew what he was thinking and she was shamed. She hung her head and whispered, 'Cut out my tongue.'

Knight leaned into Eleanor's bony chest and sucked in her smell. If he could have climbed his way around her body he would have. And she would have offered herself as his host.

The child on the sofa in the next room rumbled in his sleep. They both turned to look. Through the doorway they could see the quick up and down of his chest; it looked as if he was running in his dreams.

Eleanor's eyes were grave when she said, 'He says the soldiers who killed his father had horns and tails.' Then she looked at him and groaned; she didn't mean to, it just came out that way, 'Now you tell me how that can be?'

Knight let go of her hand, and said, 'Think about it.' And he turned to walk away.

She saw a black pit open in the floor in front of her. 'What?' she called. 'Think about what?'

He turned and spoke very quietly. 'Just think what the child would make of the world if he knew ordinary men did such things.'

# *Bastards*

Eleanor stared into those empty baked-bean tins for a long time after Knight walked away.

Like the freak winter waves at Kinlochbervie, the lives of Flambeau and Knight had sucked her into a roaring tunnel of white until she was certain she was going to die. And then they had dumped her on the hard white sand to carry on.

Knight was singing a song in Lingala when she finally followed him into the living room. The sound was deep and tender. It eased Flambeau's tortured sleep.

Eleanor watched the boy stretch out his little body and sigh softly as he dreamed.

Knight sat on the far end of the sofa. His hand rested on the boy's small feet.

What feet they were. Cracked and thick-soled and marked like a dry riverbed. Knight traced the craters with his thumb. He ran his fingers over the pitted scars in the muscle from the cobra venom and wondered at the cause.

Eleanor could see the man in Flambeau and the child in Knight.

They completed one another so well that they could have been father and son.

Knight's song petered out. He hung his head and said very quietly, 'African feet.'

She whispered, 'Aye.'

Knight pulled the blankets over Flambeau's exposed feet. Then he held out his hand to her.

She stood close beside him. He rested his head on her belly. She pushed her fingers into his hair. He looked up at her and he said, 'You got any song in you for me?'

Oh yes.


From the very first time Knight followed her hard-as-ruby nipples into her flat, Eleanor sensed she could make him happy. That her ordinary life might make it possible for him to live his less-than-ordinary one and that her body could be a raft for him to seek respite on for a time.

What she didn't know, as she led him towards her bedroom that first time, was what he could do for her.

It was uncanny that he sought out what she thought of as her short-comings and transformed them into crowning glories. He dug his long fingers into her wild Highland-cow hair and pulled. It almost hurt but didn't. It just insisted she be there, entirely, like a school bell calling her in from lunch. It said, be here with me. Be here. All of you.

And so she was. It was almost unbearable to feel the burning hunger arrive in her body. The hunger.

His fingers found the small muscles at the base of her head, the highway of feeling to her legs and her fingertips. The breasts she had always found indiscreet, he found breathtaking.

She found him so too. She kissed his glowing shoulders and felt the sinew and muscle move under her tongue. She smelt his deep smell and the rush of wet between her legs made her reach down and tear at her underwear.

'*Attends, chérie*,' he murmured in French. He told her there was no drowning dog to save. No screaming witches outside the window.

There was no hurry.

And then he leant down and sucked her nipple into his mouth. The rumble of feeling he let loose compelled her to lay open her legs and groan.

*Non!* He tucked his teeth against her nipples like a warning. She understood the unadulterated biological force drawing them together. She arched up to ask for more. He tried to hold her legs still against his chest, but she pushed him off.

She tore at her jeans. She kicked them off and with one leg still trailing she took his hand and put it between her legs.

He let out a breath that was a kind of groan, and that told her that he was as lost as she was.

He moved into her. She contracted like a clam, shook as though rigor mortis had stretched out her body – utterly involuntary, all of it.

When it was over she fell back on the bed and licked her lips.

Her eyes were almost all pupil. The light in the window beyond them hurt. This didn't happen to people like them. Did it?

This feeling of coming home?

After that, it didn't occur to her that he should ever lay his head on anyone else's pillow but hers. He married her that night in every important sense. Or rather she married him.

There was a part of him that never married her. Maybe he never would. Or could.

Flambeau woke like a firecracker in the pitch-black night. That's what happens when you fall asleep in a place that might bring trouble. You wake up firing on all cylinders.

But in Eleanor's living room late that night there was nothing but peace and the sound of Knight and her talking softly in the next room.

Flambeau crept to the door and saw them lying in bed in a post-coital glow. He wondered about adopting them forever and thereby making them his.

Knight chuckled. 'Gerry MacLean. The fisherman.' Eleanor kissed his stomach and said, 'They were all fishermen. And they all wanted my best friend, Gina. I was consolation prize.'

Eleanor pulled the sheet up to her chin, 'Gina got Gerry MacLean in the end, and a-baby-a-year.' She looked at Knight, 'And I got you.'

And as she looked at him one word came to her mind. *Hallelujah.* And with it a bubble of heat rushed into her head.

As always, Knight turned on the music and laid his clothes out on the bedcovers to dress.

Eleanor propped herself up on the cushions to watch him. She was aware that it was something of a victory each time he performed this ritual.

The people in the slum had pegged Knight and his mother as hopeless cases. They were the greater lost cause amongst the lesser lost causes.

His mother had applied her most dazzling skill and inventiveness to keeping them beautiful. And clean. She found a toilet all the way across the city where she could wash their scant clothes and wipe down their dusty bodies.

Knight would wait naked in the toilet cubicle while his single shirt and shorts dried in the hot sun outside. They shone.

His mother always told him things would get better. He believed her because it was she who said it. She found casual domestic work here and there, and with her meagre earnings she bought him two new shirts, two new shorts and a pair of red shoes.

They were her parting gift.


Eleanor lay her head back on the pillows and sighed. Knight put on a pair of elegant trousers. He turned the top of his socks over. Just so.

Eleanor closed her eyes and imagined walking down the street on his arm. She imagined people stopping to watch them pass and how they would envy her.

She felt him kiss her on the forehead and the words fell out of her mouth before she could stop them. 'Can I come with you?'

She could see immediately that her request wrongfooted him, and she wished she had caught it before it had tumbled out.

He shook his head. 'I'm going to work, *chérie*.'

'I could just watch. Tag along. I won't be a bother.'

'Work, I said.'

She should have stopped there but, once again, she didn't seem to be able to. 'It's the middle of the night. What work happens in the middle of the night?'

'Night work.'

Knight's phone beeped shrilly, signalling a text message. He ignored it. A moment of peace and then the phone screeched from his pocket.

A cell-phone rendition of 'Killing Me Softly' filled the room.

They both knew that he had to answer this one. She never knew who it was behind that particularly odious ringtone, but the sound always made Knight jump.

He extracted the phone from his pocket. '*Oui?*'

She slowly pulled the quilt over her head.

When he hung up he got down beside the bed and lifted the quilt so he could look into the cave she had made for herself under there and said, 'Got to go . . . *Blondie.*'

She blinked at him. 'Does that mean you like it? The blonde, I mean?'

'I like it. I like it.'

She smiled. 'We've got plans, right? Travel plans.'

'Plenty.'

'Okay.'

'You okay?'

'Okey-dokey.'

He smiled.

She said, 'I'm okay.'

'Good.'

He kissed her. 'Watch my homeboy.'

And then he was gone.


The possibility of sleep went with him.

Eleanor tiptoed past Flambeau on her way to the roof. She caught a glimpse of Knight as he stepped into a long black car on the street below and she watched it ease into the traffic.

She pulled her jumper closed, but she still felt the cold of the rooftop seep into her body.

'It is late.'

Eleanor turned to see Flambeau in the doorway to the roof.

'Why doesn't he ever take me with him?' she asked.

Flambeau just looked at her. How could he begin to answer that?

'Is he ashamed?'

Flambeau shook his head. He waited, hoping that would be the end of it.

'Is it because I'm not Congolese?'

Flambeau picked up an empty box of cigarettes and threw it at the chimney pot. 'I talk in Kinyarwanda when I sleep. You?'

'I don't know. English, I suppose.'

'Knight?'

Eleanor looked at him and said very quietly, 'Lingala.'

The child looked away. He didn't mean to make a point, but he saw that he had made it anyway. He sat down on the rooftop and was silent.

Eleanor looked at him, and her face was a thousand years old.

'You look cold,' said the boy gently.


The bathwater flowed over Eleanor's head. When she came up she sat very still for a moment. She could see into the bedroom through the crack in the door.

She saw Flambeau pull a sheet off the bed and send it up into the air. It floated for a moment and then it sank down to the floor. It behaved just like a sheet behaves, but that seemed to devastate the boy.

He tried again. Up. The sheet floated for a moment. His face crumpled with concentration as if he were willing it to stay up. But it returned to earth. This time Flambeau stayed under it as it fell. He looked like a snowman, or a ghost.

She called out to him. 'You still breathing under there?'

'Mama can do it.'

'What?'

'She can make it float.'

'She can?'

He nodded, his head a moving blob under the sheet. Eleanor had no idea what he was talking about so she just let it go and asked quietly, 'Why didn't she come with you to London?'

Flambeau emerged from the sheet. 'There was only money for one.'

She watched him throw the sheet in the air again, but lower this time and only to get it straight on the bed. Then he sat down on it, forlorn.

Eleanor spoke softly. 'I was younger than you are the first time I climbed out of my bedroom window and onto the roof.'

Flambeau looked up but in deference to her modesty he didn't move closer. 'The roof?'

'Of my house. I liked it up there. You could see the storms coming for miles and there was no one to talk at you.'

'You went up,' he said, 'like the sheet.'

She smiled. 'Yes, I went up. My dad followed me too.'

'Your dad like it?' asked Flambeau.

Eleanor nodded. 'He went up often after that. Once he climbed up when he was in withdrawal. The storm had hit already, but he didn't care.'

Flambeau glanced up at her and rubbed his ear. 'What's withdrawal?'

'He slipped,' said Eleanor quietly.

The two of them were so quiet that all you could hear was the drip of the water into the bath.

Then she said, 'Pity your mum wasn't there to raise him up again 'cos the whole world went to shit when he left it.'

They sat together in silence. It felt as if they were the only people left alive.

He whispered, 'No fathers.'

'Nor mothers.'

After a moment of quiet she added, 'Couple of bastards, you and me.'

Flambeau turned to look at Eleanor. It grieved him to say it, but he felt he must: 'My mother is waiting for me at Broadwater Farm.'

# Devil

The sun was already well up when Eleanor put a plate of toast on the table in front of Flambeau. She completed her offering with a cup of tea. Then she sat down to eat.

He didn't touch his breakfast.

She glanced at him.

He was wearing away at the plastic tablecloth with the blunt edge of his knife.

She asked, 'You not hungry?'

He squirmed in his chair but did not speak. She stopped eating.

He felt her stillness and looked up. 'Can we go to Broadwater Farm now?'

'Mind if I have a slice of toast first?' she said.

He shook his head and continued to saw at the tablecloth with his knife as if it were that activity alone that was keeping him alive.

She took the knife out of his hand, put it down on the table and said, 'What do you want to eat?'

He shrugged.

She said, 'I don't have any baked beans.'

He spoke very quietly. 'Salt fish.'

It was a normal thing for the child to want. He ate it for break-fast every day of his life, but it was as if he had asked her for her heart on a plate. It made her sink down into the chair.

She couldn't do salt fish.

He looked at her and then spoke. 'I made you sad.'

Eleanor saw fear and guilt travel over his face like cloud-shadows over the bare earth.

'No. It wasn't you,' she murmured gently.

Flambeau held his hands in front of him and said, 'My hands are burning.'

'What?'

Eleanor was silent as Flambeau told her that being apart from his mother made him feel as if he was being burned in a fire. It was a matter of fact and he said it just so. Every day away from her he felt the flames lick at his feet and the coals burn the palms of his hands.

Eleanor put her hands over her face. She did that because her nine-teen-year-old heart was lost somewhere in the no-man's-land between what happened in her life and what happened in his.

She might have accommodated this new window into his suffering had he given her the time. But he didn't. He looked at her with eyes fever-bright, and he added another layer. '*Moi je suis coupable.*'

He said it in French because he found it too shameful to say out loud in English.

*Cou-pa-ble* . . . the word rolled over on its own syllables and it meant BAD – plain and simple. His ten-year-old self knew with absolute certainty that all the suffering he and mother had experi-enced was his fault.

Eleanor took a long and desperate breath. She could do nothing

94

about his guilt. Nothing. She didn't have the means. It was darker and more all-consuming than she could solve.

Flambeau didn't even look up when he said, 'See.'

Eleanor stood up shakily.

He looked down into the pale palms of his hands and said, 'I make people sad.'

The truth was the child needed serious, adult, help.

Eleanor understood at that moment that she was not up to the job. 'I can't do this, Flambeau,' she whispered.

If she hadn't been in her pyjamas she would have walked Flambeau to his aunt's front door then and there in spite of his plea. 'Please let me stay. I'll make the beds. Wash the bath. I'll eat toast and tea.'

His desperation made the blood around her heart rush into her veins and arteries. Her head began to spin. She didn't know how to explain her incapacity to save his life. So she said, 'Come on, lad.'

He looked up at her.

'I'm nineteen years old and I want to go to Rome, for God's sake. I want to go to Budapest and Paris . . . and Calcutta.'

'When?' he asked. 'Today?'

'What?' she said.

'When are you going?'

She took a deep breath. 'Knight and me are going.' She turned away. 'Remember?'

It was only a hundred yards between their two front doors, but you would have thought the Sahara Desert lay between them, stinking hot and crawling with evil, the way Flambeau minded walking it.

When he had gone only a few yards he looked down into the court-yard and saw four shimmering peacock tails fanned out on the concrete quadrangle below.

He blinked to correct things, but what he saw was that his cousins all had peacock tails attached to their backs. They swished across the tar.

The cousins looked up and saw him watching and in his mind's eye they crowed, '*She's dead, freak. I bet your mother's dead.*'

Flambeau hesitated. To spur him on Eleanor called out, 'Everyone has to go home sometime, Flambeau.'

She said it to make it easier for him, but she only made it worse. Flambeau turned to look at her.

That's when she saw the light in his eyes go out.

There was a bag waiting for him outside the blue front door. He considered it warily. Kicked it gently with his foot. He opened the zip. His pyjamas were folded neatly on the top.

He knocked on the door. No one answered.

He called out, '*I'm sorry.*'

Nothing.

'*I'm sorry, Aunt.*'

But there was only silence.

He was about to turn away when the door opened just a crack and Laetitia's face appeared. She gestured to him to come closer and she whispered, '*Shsh, he will hear you.*'

Flambeau looked at her and he whispered, '*Can I come in?*'

She shook her head and said, '*Your uncle is sick.*' She reached her hand through the crack. '*He says the Devil is in you.*' She touched his cheek. '*Forgive me.*'

Someone moved in the flat behind her and she hissed, '*Go now. Go.*'

But there was nowhere else for him to go now.

Eleanor hurried onto the landing outside her kitchen door when she saw Flambeau walking away from Laetitia's with his bag over his shoulder.

'Hey, Flambeau!' she called.

He didn't stop to look at her.

'No one home?' In spite of her pyjamas she followed him out a bit further. 'You want to wait here until they come back?'

Flambeau looked at her.

She said, 'Come on.'

He cocked his head until he could see into her eyes, and then he said, 'Knight is right about you.'

He turned to go.

She followed. 'What?' Her bare feet pounded down the dirty stairs. 'What you say?'

He didn't stop. She shouted, 'Flambeau!'

He spun around and said, 'You will never know. Never know us.'

His words were bullets and they found their mark. She stepped back up a step and stumbled onto her bottom.

He slung the bag onto his shoulder and walked away down the stairs.

In a voice that had no muscle or blood she said, 'Wait for me . . .'

But Flambeau had waited long enough.

# Small Mercies

'*What kind of name is that anyway?*' Flambeau cursed under his breath as he ran across the dark black concourse and down the steep hill to the roundabout. '*El-ea-nor, sounds like a toilet flushing. Sounds like sewage,*' and he tried to wipe the loss of her from his streaming eyes.

He rode to Broadwater Farm in a taxi from the minicab office. He swore to pay the driver for the ride when he could get his hands on the small stash of notes Knight had given him and which was now hidden in a shoe at Aunt Laetitia's. That didn't work for the driver, and Flambeau was forced to make a run for it when the taxi pulled up at Broadwater Farm. The driver might have pursued the boy had it not been for the bus bristling with impatient people directly behind him at the traffic lights. As Flambeau fled he thanked God for the irate commuters therein. A brief flush of euphoria at his escape was followed by dark, jittery shame.

A wall mural – full of scenes of domestic urban bliss – covered the one wall of the Broadwater Farm housing estate. A few young men hung out on the stairs – rough kids. Flambeau had better sense than to ask them anything.

He moved on through the ground-floor parking lot underneath the buildings. He sat on the stairs.

A small wave of rowdy children swept past him. A mother yanking a child in a stroller came up, step by painful step. Flambeau would have liked to have asked her for help, but she looked so very tired.

If you grow up in London you have a feeling for the people who bear you no ill will. Those who want to make a small living and leave everyone else in peace. Those are the people you can share a stairwell with.

But if you are ten years old and from Bukavu, you don't have a way of reading the clues of the English.

As far as Flambeau was concerned, the house painter who clattered by, the teacher, the petty thief and the hooker all looked equally malevolent. The emptiness of the estate beyond them rattled him. As if the silence, too, meant him harm.

So instead of searching for his mother, he crept onto a storage shelf in the underground garage and closed his eyes. He was hiding from an as-yet-unknown hurt. It made him weep quietly with anxiety.

He didn't cry the night he hid in the cupboard under the sink in Bukavu but then his mother was with him there.

She told him a story as they crouched between the washing powder and the outflow pipe. She told it to him in whispers to stop him from calling out and giving away their hiding place.

There was a man who wanted to be king, she said. He came across three witches who told him his fortune. They said that no man who was born of woman could kill him. Flambeau laughed when he heard that. His mother put her hand over his mouth to silence him. He pulled her fingers away and said, '*Then he will never die, Mama.*'

99

'*Maybe,*' said his mother, '*maybe not.*'

Flambeau kicked her then because he couldn't stand the mystery, and it hurt to fold his body up so small and remain so still for hour after hour.

She whispered, '*Listen! Listen, Flambeau.*' She told him then that *Macbeth* was a story about how even impossible things come to pass if it is right that they do so. Flambeau knew she couldn't help sounding clever because she was a teacher. He remembered her face as she hissed, '*They do die, those that are brutal and those that are mad.*'

Flambeau could see the longing in her face when she said that.

When Flambeau looked through the crack in the cupboard door he saw his father's long, lean body standing in the doorway as if waiting for guests.

When the swaggering soldiers came with their rifles in one hand and their bottles of beer in the other he greeted them politely.

A terrible silence overtook the street after they had taken his father away. Flambeau felt the wet creep of dread and despair occupy the cupboard with them.

He asked his mother to tell him the story all over again as they waited for his father to return.

She shook her head.

Flambeau saw grief wash over her face and he knew it was because she feared he never would.

Flambeau was so lost in the memory of that night that it was as if the contents of his mind had vacated the body on the shelf in the parking garage and flown to Bukavu. He didn't even hear Eleanor as she stood in the middle of the courtyard at Broadwater Farm and called his name. 'Flambeau. Flambeau!'

If he had seen her stumbling along the pavement, one foot in front of the other, he would have realised she was undone with distress at his flight.

He would have heard her befuddlement as she asked the policeman for directions with the words falling out of her mouth in the wrong order. He would have seen her repeat them more slowly to arrive at, 'Sorry, can you tell me how I can get to Broadwater Farm?'

He would have known she cared.

But he didn't know that, and so Flambeau waited for the safety of the evening bustle of those returning from work and school before he emerged onto the open concourse in the centre of the estate.

People ebbed and flowed around him as they made their way to their front doors, or to the bus stop on the street. He glanced at each face to see if it was his mother.

He looked until the concourse was empty once more.

It was pitch-dark before he turned and walked, defeated, across the vacant courtyard.


Three phones were ringing in the minicab office and the radio was baying out frantic messages, but Eleanor ignored it all except for the landlord on line four.

His abuse made her lean her head on the desk. She wanted to curse him but instead she bit the inside of her cheek and said, 'Mr Leighton . . . I will pay you the rent on Friday, I swear.'

The line went dead and she rolled her head to the side and stared at the image of her wasted face in the silver kettle.

When the Postman swept into the office with his usual good cheer, she was ashen. 'Please go away,' she murmured.

'What's with you?' Postman asked, perplexed.

She didn't mean to tell him anything, but the kindness in his enquiring face just opened the floodgates. 'Flambeau is gone,' she blurted.

'What?'

'I tried to find him, but he's gone. I don't even know how to tell Knight. He's gone too. Everybody is gone.'

The Postman looked at her for what seemed like a long time. She let her misery wash over her without censor.

It moved the Postman enough for him to offer her what he could by way of comfort. 'Knight will come,' he said.

She looked at him.

'He may not be able to come now, this minute, but he will come and he will find the child.'

'How do you know that?' said Eleanor.

'Because I know him.'

She spoke softly. 'Do I know him? I mean . . . do you think I do?'

He glanced at her. 'Do you even know his name?'

'Knight?' she said.

'I mean his given name, his family name?'

She shook her head.

'Do you want to know?'

She looked at him and she whispered, 'Please.'

The Postman considered her, then he spoke slowly. 'He is Tresor Sese Yakoko. His mother's name was Biti Yakoko.'

Eleanor lowered her head and felt the sound of those names wind themselves around her insides and she said, 'Thank you.'

'They say his father was the inspector of schools for the Great Lakes Region. He didn't stay long enough to give the boy his name.' Postman sat on the orange plastic chair with a sigh. 'His mother was just a schoolgirl when they met.'

Eleanor looked at him and said gently, 'And what is your name?'

He shrugged. 'Postman.'

'Your real one.'

He shook his head. Like Knight, he had a kind of *nom de plume* for his activities in London. His role in Knight's small cabal entailed stealing forgeable cheques from the Royal Mail, where he had a part-time day job. So Postman he became.

Eleanor looked at him and said quietly, 'Your real name?'

Postman smiled and waved away her question. 'Ah no.'

'Come on, spill the beans,' she said.

'You won't laugh?' he asked.

'I swear.'

He looked down into his hands and said, 'Pacifique.'

'Pacifique?'

'My mother named me Pacifique so I would be calm in the face of life's many storms.' Postman rubbed his chin and mumbled, 'And then she died.'

He smiled wryly.

If she had known him just a little better Eleanor would have hugged him to her chest and groaned at the pathos in his face, but she was Scottish so she simply looked at him and said, 'Tea?'

He nodded. 'Strong, black . . .'

'It's a beautiful name.'

She clattered the cups and brought the water to a boil. As she poured the milk she whispered to herself, 'Tresor Sese Yakoko.'

She meant it to be silent, but he heard her and smiled. 'He is Knight now.'

'Now who gave him that name?'

'I did.' Postman knew he could never tell Eleanor how Tresor became Knight. His silence was his gift to her.

The very first time Postman said it, it came out of his mouth in English. *Knight*. And so it remained.

Knight marked his mother's grave with a Coke bottle so he could always find her. That's what he was doing when Postman first saw him.

As part of his initiation into his new family of vagabonds and thieves he was given the task of burning Mama Kasavubu's hut. Everyone said she was a witch because there had been some bad luck in the neighbourhood. Knight didn't believe in witches. And it seemed like there was always bad luck in Ndjili.

He had to set the hut alight and watch it burn to embers. He was not permitted to look away even when he thought he saw the shape of the old lady herself, even then.

Maybe it was because Knight ended up on his side in a pool of his own vomit, but still looking, that Postman got his full measure. It was then that he named him Knight.

Postman knew there were many who did such things lightly. But not Knight. In fact he should have. By all accounts, by anyone's measure, he was destined for that. But Knight became something else.

The back of Flambeau's head was as spongy as dark moss and infinitely lonely as he sat on the park bench in the growing dusk.

He dug in his bag for something to eat. If he was lucky, his aunt would have stuffed a piece of bread down the side of the bag.

His blue pyjamas landed on the bench beside him. A pair of socks, a jersey, a long-sleeved T-shirt, a toothbrush, a worn winter jacket.

Then Flambeau found the photograph of his mother that used to sit on the wall above his bed. He looked at it closely, then he laid it on the bench. Oh, and the business card from the minicab place. All of that had meaning for the boy, but meaning fades when you are hungry.

He got up and walked away from it all. He stopped, turned, went back for the photograph, slipped it in his pocket, and then he laid himself down under the furthest bench.

Flambeau's attempt to hide in the slim shadow of the bench was so despairing that a mother with three children hanging off her pushchair stopped to look. She saw no other children in the park at this hour.

The mother knocked on the window of the park attendant's small hut and woke him from his indolent stupor.

She didn't have to do that. Neither did the park attendant have to wander over to talk to the child lying under the bench. Flambeau rolled over onto his side and closed his eyes when the attendant told him he should go home.

Then he saw the flotsam of Flambeau's life on the park bench and assumed he was a runaway. He found the business card on the bench and he used his pay-as-you-go to phone the minicab office. Eleanor was away from her desk and one of the drivers was manning the phones. He didn't know anything about a boy.

'I'm going to lock up now, lad. You got somewhere to go?' the park attendant shouted over to Flambeau.

Flambeau didn't even look up.

'You can't stay here.'

Flambeau covered his head with his arms to block out the sound.

The park attendant sighed. 'If I phone the police I'll get home at midnight and God knows what will happen to you.'

'Please. Not the police.' Flambeau was on his feet.

'What then?'

Flambeau had no idea.

The attendant tried the number one more time. This time Eleanor picked up.

Later, when it was over, she said, 'Thank God he did that.'

Thank God for the small and tender mercies that attend lives like these.


It was pitch-dark when Eleanor's double shift ended and she came to get Flambeau. She hurried down the long deserted road to the park gates where the small boy waited on a bench. She sat beside him. Neither of them spoke. Then she said, 'Sorry.'

He didn't answer. He looked down at his hands. He wanted to say sorry too. He wanted to say sorry for telling her she knew nothing. He wanted to tell her that he needed her, but he feared that any word from him might change her mind about taking him home.

Eleanor waited. Then she said it again. 'I'm sorry.'

She got up to walk.

Flambeau followed.

And so they made their way through the dark until the roar of the night traffic on Tottenham High Street swallowed up the sound of their feet.

# *Fatima*

Eleanor took two tins of baked beans out of her handbag. 'I thought you might be hungry.'

Flambeau smiled. He watched her prise open the lids and empty them into a pot on the stove. He was grave with anticipation.

She put the steaming bowl of baked beans down on the small table.

Flambeau lifted his fork, paused, then lowered it again. He wanted to eat, but his hunger had been too protracted and he could no longer do it.

She murmured, 'You can try again later.'

The key sounded in the lock and without turning to see, she said, 'Nice of you to show up.'

There was no answer so Eleanor continued, 'I offered him beans, but the poor lad's stomach is the size of a pea.'

Then she heard Knight say, 'This is Fatima.'

She swung around to see a young Sudanese woman in a burkha standing in her kitchen, clearly terrified.

Eleanor got to her feet. Flambeau followed. Everyone was silent, then Eleanor said, 'Hello.'

The woman called Fatima was too scared to respond. Knight told them she didn't speak English.

'What does she speak?' asked Flambeau.

'I don't know.' Knight took off his jacket. 'But she needs a place to stay tonight.'

Eleanor said, 'Oh.' And she looked at him.

Flambeau walked over and took the small suitcase from Fatima's hand. He looked at Eleanor and said, 'I think she's hungry.'

'Yeah,' said Knight.

'She probably doesn't want baked beans,' murmured Eleanor.

'No.'

'No. Okay.'

Eleanor opened the kitchen cupboard. A packet of tea and a box of cocoa powder stared back at her.

'There's salt fish under the sink,' said Knight, and he put a plastic bag on the table. 'Cassava.'

'Right.' Eleanor reached for the frying pan and put it on the gas, poured oil into it.

She scared herself, the way she clattered and clanked the pans. Her voice shook with feeling as she asked, 'Where've you been, Knight?'

Flambeau led Fatima away from the small fracas he could see building in the kitchen. They sat side by side on the sofa, two stolen birds, and listened to Eleanor turn her good name to ashes in the kitchen.

'I lost Flambeau . . . in fact . . . the whole bloody world was coming to an end and I couldn't find you!'

Eleanor took the salt fish out of its plastic bag and then she paused.

It was a weird-looking thing, flat and wide and dry as a bone. Knight had the good sense to take it from her and cut it into pieces. 'Get the chilli.'

'You get the bloody chilli.'

'You want rent money. This pays,' he snapped.

That's when she stopped to look at him. 'That poor girl pays you?'

'No.' And he spat, 'Red chilli.'

She couldn't have moved to get his blasted chilli even if she had wanted to.

He chopped at the fish once more. 'I sometimes pick an illegal up from here and I drop them there and they pay me.'

He looked at her. And she at him. 'Who pays you?'

He brought the knife down hard enough to split the wooden board and spat, 'Just make me a decent fish pondu . . .'

She looked at him and breathed out the word, 'Deo.'

Knight whipped around to look at her and shouted, '. . . or is that too much to ask?'

Flames and smoke billowed from the frying pan. Knight turned to swat at the flames with a dishcloth, 'Shit. Shit. Shit.'

She grabbed the frying pan out of his hands and snapped, 'What's next?'

Knight looked at her.

'What's next after the fucking chilli?'

'Fry the onions and manioc, add the fish.'

'Now get out.'

'You going do this on your own?'

'Get out.'

He turned away from her fury, but the sight of Flambeau in the living room with his hands over his ears to keep out their fighting stopped him short.

Fatima spoke to the boy in gentle Arabic. Flambeau couldn't understand a word, but somehow the sound of the words comforted him.

He leant against Fatima's arm, she shifted slightly to accommodate him.

Knight called softly, '*Chérie.*'

Eleanor didn't want to hear him. She swept across the doorway on her way to the sink but a glimpse of the tenderness between the two lost souls on the sofa gave her pause.

Eleanor took a deep breath and murmured, 'His mother will come and it will be all right.'

Knight looked at her. It was a quiet and fearful glance, but he said nothing.

'Right? I mean someone will come,' she said.

Knight turned back into the kitchen and said, 'His mother will never come.' He spoke with quiet certainty, 'They will keep her until she's all used up and no one wants her any more. Then they'll throw her into the street.'

Eleanor looked at him for an eternity, trying to grasp what he had just said. 'And this woman? Here? Fatima?'

He spoke very quietly. 'I don't think she'll ever make it home again.'

'Jesus!' shouted Eleanor.

'Yes.' He grabbed a chilli from the basket next to the stove and began to chop it furiously.

She watched him. 'We've got to go to the police.'

'If you want me to go to jail. Yes. Go.'

'Why would you go to jail?'

'Because I brought her here.'

Eleanor had to sit down for a moment, or she would have fallen.

He looked at her and said very quietly, 'You see how it is with us?' He shook his head. 'The boy has no one.' He wiped his hand over his face. '*Tu vois, chérie?*'

Silence. She looked up at him, tired. 'Aye, I see.'

And then she got up and walked to the window: she didn't seem to be able to get enough air into her lungs. She pushed open the window and then said, 'Just tell me I'm not going to end up back in Kinlochbervie filleting fish to keep him alive.'

Knight laughed and looked up. But her eyes were brimming, 'While you swan around London doing God-knows-what in the middle of the night dressed like John fucking Travolta in *American Gigolo*.' She had to take another breath then. 'Or was it Richard Gere?'

'Who?'

'You've never seen it, have you?'

He shook his head.

'It was on TV one Christmas Eve. It's a great movie. And your life is just . . . nothing . . . without it . . .' She turned away and mumbled into her chin, 'Like mine would be without you.'

He touched her mouth, to shut her up, tender as a breeze. She closed her eyes to feel it, but it burnt and she bit her lip so as not to cry out.

A rustle at the door and both were aware of the presence of someone there. Their heads turned as one head.

Flambeau stood in the doorway. His face a shade paler with anxiety.

No one spoke.

Then Eleanor said quietly, 'You want to stay here with us a while, Flambeau?'

Flambeau looked at her, then at Knight.

The smallest trace of a one-sided smile curled at the corner of Flambeau's mouth. Eleanor turned to the stove. 'Now get out, the both of you.' She picked up a ladle and said, 'I am going to make some of the salt fish pondu . . . for which I will soon be famous.'

★

A lone candle in a jam jar burnt on the table. Everyone had a serving of cassava and pondu in front of them. No one seemed very sure who should start. Fatima mumbled a prayer under her breath and then tentatively scooped the cassava up in her fingers.

All eyes were on her.

She dipped her hand in the food once again and scooped up another mouthful. She loved it. Oh thank God. The very air lit up.

Flambeau laughed. 'I think she likes it.'

Eleanor said, 'I think she might.'

Knight was the big surprise. 'I like it.'

Nothing had ever made Eleanor feel as good as hearing those words.

Fatima came up for air and saw them all watching her. She put her hands together and bowed her head.

# Music

The early morning light barely dented the darkness in the living room where Fatima waited. She sat on the sofa, head covered in her shawl, fully dressed.

Knight came into the room. He picked up her suitcase without a word. Neither one looked at the other.

Knight saw Flambeau's clothes laid out on the back of the sofa in direct mimicry of his own morning dressing ritual. He smiled fleetingly. Then he saw the photograph of Flambeau's mother laid out there too, like a declaration. He picked it up.

Bijou's vivid face laughed out at him. She was so alive, so seamlessly bonded to the small boy by her side. Eastern Congo's lush green all around them.

The sight of her caught Knight in his throat.

'*She was not at Broadwater Farm.*' Flambeau's voice startled him. '*I looked there.*'

Knight glanced down at Flambeau's small face on the sofa. He turned away from the boy and muttered, '*Sorry to hear that, brother.*'

Fatima followed Knight to the door. Flambeau slipped out of his sofa bed and beat them to it. '*Where is she going?*'

Knight didn't look at him when he said, '*To get a good job so she can feed her children at home.*'

'*How many children?*'

'*Three or four.*'

'*How old are they?*'

'*I don't know.*'

'*When will they see her again?*'

'*Soon.*'

When Flambeau kissed Fatima's hand she laughed and modestly withdrew it, then quickly ruffled his hair to ease his hurt.

The boy watched from the window as she walked with Knight across the courtyard and got into his car.

Flambeau turned back into the empty room. It felt eerily silent. He called out softly, 'Eleanor?'

'Mmmmm,' came the reply. She was counting the coins in her hand as she shuffled into the living room in her slippers.

He could see she was trying to keep track, 'Twenty-five, twenty-six, twenty-seven . . .'

He watched her turn over the glass bowl on the table and begin to count the coins she found there. 'I'm thirty bloody pounds short,' she said.

'For what?'

She sighed, 'The rent,' and she shuffled off into the passage, 'Mr-Leighton-the-landlord will evict us if he doesn't get it today.'

She said it as if 'the-landlord' were part of his name too.

Flambeau didn't need to look in his pockets to know he had no money. The little he did have was in his shoe, and that was in the flat occupied by Didier and his devil.

The child did what he always did when he was lost. He sang. It was a slight, uncertain, childhood song, but it was all he could do just then.

Music had saved him from despair many times, but the first time his mother showed him its power was the one he remembered best.

It happened on a truck. Flambeau and his mother were returning from a visit to her parental home in Minembwe on the High Plateau. It was late.

Through the slits of his tired eyes Flambeau watched the setting sun bounce on the horizon as the truck tipped in and out of potholes on the rutted road.

Flambeau leant against his mother's arm. The sacks of cassava on which they had sat for close to seven hours had moulded to their tired bodies. Flambeau's eyes began to close.

The woman sitting across from him was a neighbour from Bukavu who had watched him grow from nothing. She was a good woman. She smiled at him and he smiled back sleepily.

She had a chicken in a dry-grass cage on her lap. She was going to cook it when she got home. Flambeau dreamt of the smell it would make while it was cooking.

He remembered thinking that his mother's smell was even better than roast chicken. She smelled of lemons and the wild honeysuckle that grew on the edge of their yard. It was the smell of sanctuary.

He was so deeply, safely asleep on his sack of cassava that he wasn't aware when the shouts from the forest began. The woman with the chicken screamed with such undisguised horror that it wrenched Flambeau back from sleep. In its wake the truck's ancient brakes sounded to him like hogs squealing.

His mother grabbed his hand and pulled him down under the sack of cassava on which they sat. She pulled so hard it felt as if his arm was being torn out of its socket. He felt someone pushing from behind him and he turned to see the chicken woman, her face contorted with the effort of forcing his soft body between the less-soft sacks.

The two women burrowed silently, headfirst. They seemed to understand one another perfectly. Arms and shoulders worked together in a reptilian sideways motion to force out space for their passage. When they were hidden from sight they turned their bodies and kicked out a small cave with their feet.

Flambeau clung to his mother in the tiny pocket of air and listened to the screams beyond. They were like nothing he had ever heard before.

Male voices sounded very close. Shouting. The wall of their cave shifted as someone walked over the top of it.

Drops of sweat gathered on Bijou's forehead and then trickled down into her eyes. He wondered why she didn't wipe them away and then he saw that the only thing holding up the roof of their small cave was her sinewy arms. If she let them rest, even for a moment, the weight of the full sacks above would crush them.

Flambeau reached up and wiped the sweat off her forehead with the back of his arm.

The voices retreated and the chicken woman began to mutter a prayer. Flambeau and his mother joined her. They knew only God and the ancestors stood between them and the cries they heard alongside them.

His mother's arms had begun to shake uncontrollably by the time the shrieking quieted. The two women nodded to one another and then began their journey back up to the surface.

His mother held Flambeau's face close to her body as they climbed off the truck. He could feel her begin to keen. She stood beside the truck on the red dust of the road and the grief at what she saw ran through her body like lava.

She held him tight against her to protect him from seeing what she saw, but every instinct in the boy wanted to see, needed to see. She held firm. Flambeau glimpsed a small river of red make its way along the dust. He saw a shoe that lay on the earth without its owner. Someone's still arm rested at an impossible angle against the tyre of the truck.

Then Flambeau did not want to see any more. He could feel a tightness growing around his chest and just when he thought there was no longer room for another breath in there and that he would surely die, his mother began to sing.

And as she sang, she walked away from the blood. She walked and she sang, and with every word and every note he could feel life coming back to him. He felt the future. And the future was in the music and it was in her. It was better than a kidney transplant when you are dying. It was magic.

Flambeau sat on Eleanor's carpet in his pyjamas and his song came to an end. In the silence that followed, he heard the sound of her turning out all the jars, bowls, pockets and drawers in her bedroom.

He heard the clink of coins being counted and her cursing under her breath. It was the sound of precariousness, and he knew it well. Money was the only thing between him and the park bench, the underground garage, or worse . . .

He was on his feet and out of the door before he had time to consider the danger of his mission. If he had, he would almost certainly have remained crouched on the carpet to wait for whatever fate had in store for him.

★

The sun felt hot on the dark brick wall under his old bedroom window. He pushed his bare knees against it and listened with his ear up against the glass for any movement beyond. He was oblivious to the fact that he was still in his pyjamas. His cousins would have gone to school long ago. His aunt and uncle tended to do their errands early in the day.

Flambeau pulled himself up onto the window ledge. The small top window was open as usual. He began to lift himself up to it. He sucked in his breath and pulled himself through, inch by inch. As he did so he remembered his recent escape for the same window to follow Knight down the hill. It seemed like a lifetime ago. In the distance he heard Eleanor call his name. Or did he?

He exhaled and pulled himself up one more inch. And then one more. Just as he felt his ribs bend dangerously against the pressure of the window frame, he slid onto the floor like a baby giraffe, born slick with fear.

Silence. The beds were unmade. Shoes and clothes scattered. It looked like the people who lived there had leapt out of bed and run for their lives. That's what it looked like to him.

Flambeau crawled over to the cupboard in the corner of the room, and there, under a mountain of shoes and bags, he saw his old school shoe, worn from black to grey. He pulled it out and shoved his hand inside it.

Thirty-three pounds and fifty pence lay on his palm. Hallelujah. His fingers closed around it.

Then he heard a breath. It wasn't his breath. It was a sigh. The way the air shook as it came out made him think of an old person.

He peered further and further into the doorway so he could see the source of the sound. It was empty.

'Flambeau,' Eleanor called from the walkway some doors down,

'Flambeau!' Her voice rang out again, closer now, the sound echoed inside the room.

Before the child had the chance to answer, a wraith appeared in the doorway.

Flambeau had seen how hardship could shape and change a person. He knew it never came without a cost, but this transformation was like no other. It sucked the light out of his eyes to see it.

His Uncle Didier wore only a pair of faded boxer shorts. He moved as if he and his spectrally thin body were no longer connected. As if his feet and his head were operated by different beings.

Flambeau sucked in a breath, involuntarily.

The wraith paused, rocked slightly on his feet like a praying mantis. Then he turned and shuffled on. His footfall sounded far too light.

Then Flambeau saw the string that was tied around his uncle's waist. Flambeau's eyes followed the string from the man's stomach along the floor and to the doorknob of the bedroom. He was tied up like a goat would be in their backyard in Bukavu. The boy guessed the string served to stop his uncle wandering out of the house and into the cruel world beyond it.

The blue nylon string had worn away the brown of Didier's skin in places, revealing the pink and tender muscle underneath. Flambeau groaned quietly.

A terrible and unexpected love filled the boy. He rested his head on the floorboards to ease his sudden vertigo. He would never have known to use the word compassion to describe the feeling, but that's what it was.

Flambeau sank back into the shadows of the room. When his uncle's footsteps had faded and a sad silence had taken their place,

Flambeau got up slowly. He stood in the dark room for a moment.

Then he jumped onto the sill and slithered out of the small window. It was as if, this time, his body had narrowed and grown scales in preparation for life in the water.

He collided with Eleanor as he ran around the corner. They both had all the air knocked out of their lungs. He thought she resembled a goldfish as she sucked it back in, then she said, 'Lord, child. Where were you?'

Flambeau held out the money.

'What's this?'

Flambeau looked at her and blinked. 'The rent.'

'Oh Jesus. Where did you get it?'

'From inside my shoe.'

'Your shoe . . . (she pointed to his old home) . . . in there?'

He nodded. She looked at him. Flambeau smiled. 'Say thank you.'

'Thank you!' She grabbed him and hugged him so close he could hardly breathe. She kissed him on each of his closed eyes and then she laughed.

Flambeau pushed the play button on Knight's blaster with the confidence of the triumphant hero. Eleanor was at the small table, her back to him, doing a final count.

Music filled the room. Flambeau threw off his pyjamas and finally dressed for the day, item by item, to the sound of Papa Wemba.

First he donned his socks, then his skinny grey shorts. Then his white shirt and school tie with stretchy elastic round the neck. He had the makings of a real style fiend even though his current attire begged improvement.

When he was dressed, he stuffed his mother's photograph into his shorts without looking at it.

Just then Eleanor turned to him, grinning, and said, 'You did it. We've got the rent!'

Flambeau laughed and did a two-step, then a turn with perfect form.

Eleanor laughed when she said, 'You're going to have to teach me to dance like that.'

'You want to dance?' he asked somewhat warily.

'I want to dance like that.'

Flambeau had seen her and Knight do a sort of Rhumba that day, long ago, as he waited for his mother. It looked to him like the movement began in her head instead of in her body. He wondered if it was because she came from a cold place? He remembered how Knight had winked at him as they danced as if to say *She can't be what she is not*. It did not bode well for the Rhumba.

Eleanor held out her hands to him. 'Teach me now.'

Flambeau looked as if he was going to have his teeth pulled.

They didn't make an auspicious start. At first she thought it was her level of skill that made Flambeau move so half-heartedly. Then she wondered if it had something to do with his age. Maybe he just didn't want to get close?

He shook his head and stopped moving altogether.

'Sorry. Am I doing something wrong?' she asked.

'You are thinking,' he murmured.

'Thinking?'

'Turn off your head switch.'

'Right.' She mimed turning a switch behind her ear. That got a small smile out of him.

*One . . . three, four, one . . . three four*, he clapped, and then he moved one leg. He clapped the rhythm again and moved the other leg, *one . . . three, four, one . . . three four*.

As he danced she could see him begin to lose himself in the movement. He bent his knees. His upper body moved hardly at all while his legs and hips switched and curled underneath him. She applauded. He reached out his hand and endeavoured to lead her through the simple sequence. It ended badly.

'I think I might need another lesson or two,' she said sheepishly.

The idea clearly didn't please Flambeau.

'When you get back from school tomorrow maybe?' she suggested.

'School?'

'School.'

She nodded and said it again. 'School.' Now that Flambeau was staying with her, Eleanor half expected someone from social services to bang on their door and ask what had become of him.

That's what they did up in Kinlochbervie if a child didn't show up to her dad's school. More often than not they would find him or her on a family-owned lobster boat, worn to a ravelling from days of labour.

Eleanor wondered if it was different in London, where there were more kids missing than in class. Immigrant kids anyway. The ones like Flambeau who nobody expected would make it through to the other side.

'I will go to school when I have found my mother.' Flambeau spoke with quiet certainty.

Eleanor turned to look at him so suddenly that he felt the air shift around her. She wanted to tell him what Knight had told her. That he should give up on ever finding his ma. That it would be better for him just to build a life without her. But she could not.

The doorbell rang.

They didn't often have guests, so when the bell rang it was more likely to bring trouble than joy.

Eleanor opened the door reluctantly.

Postman nodded a greeting from the doorstep. Eleanor smiled.

'You okay?' he asked.

'Okay.'

Both stood there awkwardly for a moment then she said, 'Knight's not here.'

She could tell he was disappointed and so she asked him in for tea.

His face brightened.

Eleanor stepped aside. As Postman entered he said he liked the faded poodle on her pyjama bottoms.

She looked down and said, 'Is that what it is? I always thought it was a cloud.'

He reconsidered it and said in the way only an African could, 'A poodle becomes a cloud simply through repeated washing.'

She laughed. It was a good sound.

Postman followed her through into the lounge and saw Flambeau at the window.

Eleanor carried on through the living room and into the kitchen.

Postman hovered near the boy. '*Hey, Homeboy.*'

Flambeau nodded as if Postman's presence there was as natural as daylight. He said, in Lingala, '*Fatima is back.*'

'What about Fatima?' said Eleanor as she came into the room, tea tray in hand. 'Bugger, I forgot the digestives. Can you grab them, lad?'

Flambeau ran off to do her bidding. She slid the tray onto the table and crossed over to the window.

Eleanor saw Fatima get into a long black car. Then the man who was holding the door open turned, and Eleanor saw that it was Deo.

'What's he doing here?' she spat. She looked at Postman. 'What does he want?'

'Who?'

'Deo.'

Postman turned away.

Eleanor could see that he knew but was not telling. That's when she said his name, out loud, 'Pacifique!'

No one had used that name for as long as he could remember. It was ancient, his response to it involuntary. He looked at her.

She asked it again. 'Why is he here?'

Postman scanned Eleanor's face. He sat down in the hard plastic chair and sighed. 'Because we owed him something.'

She leant against the glass and whispered, 'What?'

Postman glanced at her but said nothing. Eleanor turned back to the window in time to see Deo's long black car slide into the main road like an eel. She whispered, 'Fatima. You owed him Fatima.'

She turned to look at Postman with such dawning horror that Postman whispered. 'No choice—'

Flambeau came back with the biscuits. Postman could see Eleanor was in no shape to pour the tea, so he did it. He added sugar for them all and handed her a cup.

Knight burst through the door at just that moment. He brought a fiery blast of defeat with him.

Postman turned. '*Where have you been, brother?*'

'*Out.*'

'*Out where?*' insisted Postman.

'*Just out.*'

Postman shook his head. '*Deo was not happy.*'

'*Fuck him,*' said Knight.

'*No thanks.*'

Knight kicked open the kitchen door and stepped inside it. '*I was at the mosque.*'

'*What?*'

'*The mosque. She wanted to go to the mosque on her last day. Okay?*' and he slammed the kitchen door closed behind him.

Postman sat down at the tea table. He ran his fingers over his hair. Eleanor looked at him and mouthed, *What is he saying*?

Postman shook his head. 'He took her to the mosque.'

Eleanor sucked in a breath.

'*Is that okay with you, Mister Postman?*' shouted Knight from behind the closed door.

Flambeau looked up, frightened by the anger in his friend's voice and completely at sea as to why it should be so. Eleanor flew across the room to Flambeau's side and took his hand.

It was a good thing she did that because neither she nor Flambeau had ever seen a sight as frightening as the despair and fear on Knight's face as he blasted open the kitchen door and shouted at Postman, '*Is it? Because if it isn't, all I can say is FUCK YOU, brother.*'

# Jacob's Ladder

Like all nine-year-old boys let loose in the African bush, Flambeau and his best friend Pelo loved to see how close they could get to death's door without actually stepping through to the other side.

They had been told never to wade in the shallows of Lake Kivu or fall asleep on its luscious banks. They were warned of a gas that came up from under the water to steal away your life. And indeed, one drunken neighbour, on his way home from a wedding party, had curled up for a nap and had never woken again.

So Pelo and Flambeau lay in the deepest crevasse, which they imagined contained the most noxious fumes, and sucked in as much poisonous air as they could. They courted death just long enough to acquit themselves and then burst up, gasping.

Then they laughed.

It was a drunken, unkeeled sound that meant *We are still alive*.

The atmosphere in the flat after Fatima left seemed to Flambeau to be just as toxic as the gas from Lake Kivu. The three of them walked around on eggshells.

When Flambeau went to pee in the middle of the night he found

Eleanor sitting on the toilet. Not using it. Just sitting. Grey-skinned. Haunted.

He would have liked to have taken her hand and asked her what was troubling her. But when she turned to look at him, Flambeau saw a furious, inward disquiet in her eyes. And he fled.

Then Knight disappeared for four straight days and nights.

On the first day of his disappearance Eleanor and Flambeau moved stoically through their ordinary domestic routine. She told herself that Knight had done this before. He would be back.

By the end of the second day Eleanor felt as if her skin was beginning to peel off. She itched. She lay on the sofa and stuffed her hands under her body to keep herself from scratching. She sent Flambeau to ask Postman where Knight was. Then she went onto the roof to watch for his return.

Her mother's voice inside her head said Knight had buggered off and that it served her right for loving him in the first place.

Her father's voice warned of the dangers of being there when he came back: *Now he's a lot to take on, young Eleanor lass. Maybe you should pack your bags and go home.*

What those parental voices really ought to have been saying was that it takes compassion and courage to love someone when you didn't see too much of that yourself. And then they should have said they were sorry for failing her thus. But they were both dead to her and so they never would.

The rays of evening sunlight hit the empty centre of the rooftop at such an extreme angle that it looked as if they originated from the floor and not the sky.

The uneasy luminosity drew Eleanor away from her place of vigil on the edge of the building.

As she stood in the centre of the glowing, empty space she began to count inside her head, *one . . . three, four, one . . . three four*. Just as Flambeau had taught her.

In this way, and very slowly, she began to dance the Rhumba.

She was stilted and wooden.

If Flambeau had seen her he would have told her to turn her head-switch off. But this uninspired, mechanical movement was all there was between her and despair. She didn't care how it looked as long as it quieted her raucous insides.

As she moved, her body remembered dancing with Knight on their first night out. He had taken her to a small Congolese nightclub.

She had never heard music like the Rhumba before. It filled her up from her toes to her head. It made her shake and gasp and when she caught sight of herself in the mirror, she was someone else.

Even though she was a hopeless dancer compared to just about everyone in the room, she felt loose and easy for the first time. Like someone raised in a hot country.

Afterwards, Knight walked her up the dirty stairs to the fake-wood front door of her council flat. She would always remember how the words 'Goodnight lassie', spoken in ironic French-African English, tripped off his tongue. Then he turned to go.

She reached out into the dark night that threatened to suck him away and took his arm. She could tell he was surprised. He turned and looked at her.

She didn't usually show her teeth but she shot him through the heart with that smile. Her dad used to say it was a weapon of mass destruction, her smile, much looked for, rarely found, but deadly when deployed.

Knight cocked his head but he didn't smile back. He just reached over and touched her nipple with his long fingers and she could feel a burning in her knickers and a rushing in her blood.

She knew that all she had to do was turn around and walk back into the house and there was no power on earth that could keep him from following her. She had him. It is a dangerous thing when a young woman first glimpses that power.

It had brought Knight back to her every day since then. Against all the odds.

Eleanor stopped dancing and she stood in the middle of the vast roof.

She wondered whether it would bring him back this time.

Knight showed up two days later. He walked into the apartment as if he'd just popped out to buy milk. As if he hadn't had them all fearing the worst for four stinking days.

Postman was at the kitchen table drinking a cup of tea when Knight breezed in. He had been there for the last three mornings. Just in case of crisis. He did a lot of things *just in case*.

Knight swept past his oldest friend without a word.

He tousled Flambeau's head. Then he saw Eleanor. He hesitated for a moment, uncertain. He could see the mark of his absence on her face.

She got shakily to her feet.

She was only half up and out of her chair when he swept her into his arms. Nobody could have said whether it was a laugh or a cry that came out of her mouth when he lifted her.

Knight carried her into the bedroom and kicked the door closed behind him.

Flambeau looked at his hands as if to reassure himself that he was still there. He had been made invisible by Knight's perfunctory acknowledgement.

Knight had the power to do that.

The boy could see that Postman was equally bereft, but he had managed that feeling for longer so he simply sighed and took another sip of tea.

Flambeau murmured, 'He should eat something.'

Postman coughed and said, 'He'll eat later.' Intimate laughter from the bedroom propelled Postman and Flambeau to their feet. They were both suspended there: uncomfortable, unsure what to do next.

'Come,' Flambeau said. And he led Postman to the door.

In the shadows of the dark bedroom Eleanor took Knight's face into her hands. The eagerness in her trembling fingers shamed her.

The truth was that even if Knight had played a part in Fatima's terrible fate, it did not stop Eleanor from holding his head and quivering.

Such was her hunger.

She whispered, 'You came back.'

He laughed then, with a light toss of his head, and said, 'Always.'

The ease with which he said it inflamed her still-aching insides. 'Always?' she whispered.

How did he know that? Really? Did he know how fearful she had been that he wouldn't return?

Did he know that she lived with that fear not only when he disappeared for long stretches but *every bloody day*?

She looked at him and could see that he didn't. He didn't know. His obliviousness to this most basic condition of their love made new crevasses of loneliness in her.

She wanted to cry. He reached for her. She wanted to laugh. A profound rage replaced her relief at his return.

She drove her fingernails into his back. And he howled.

He pinned her arms by her side, vice-grip-tight, and he hissed, '*No, chérie. No!*'

But no wasn't enough.

She bit him in his shoulder and he reared away from her. But he was back quick as lighting. Kissing her. His ardour sucked the sting out of her gut.

His colonisation of her body swept them into the final ravaging communion they hungered for and could find with no one else.

Afterwards she lay on her side, her back to him. She heard him breathe beside her. It occurred to her then that they could live this way only for so long before they followed one another into madness.

'*See?*' Flambeau laughed. '*This is the swift.*' Postman allowed Flambeau to deposit the bird on his finger. Its tiny claws gripped tight. Postman smiled.

'Come. There is more,' said the child.

Flambeau showed Postman the rest of the roof as if he were an estate agent showing off his one great asset. Then he led him to the corner where the sun was always warmest. And they sat.

That's when Flambeau the master strategist dug out his Jacob's ladder. The paper was worn soft with use, more like thin animal hide than parchment.

He handed it to Postman and watched while he read: *boat, hospitel, plan air, train, polic, ship, aliv e, tran staton, lost*. There was a tick against *polic*.

*Morgue* was still written on the bottom, and it was still spelt *M-O-R-G*. When Postman had finished reading he looked up at Flambeau and he said quietly, '*Where are we going to find a boat, my brother?*'

Flambeau shrugged. He avoided Postman's doubting gaze. He was hoping he would be a believer. Flambeau took the paper back and began to fold it. Postman watched him tuck it into his back pocket and then he said, '*But I saw a hospital on the corner by Sterling Road.*'

Flambeau looked up at him and grinned.

Nobody took any notice of the man with a young boy at his side as they walked into the hospital foyer.

Postman hesitated at the information desk, but the harried woman manning it looked as if she could cause him some trouble so he took Flambeau's arm and floated across the hallway and into the open lift. It went up.

They followed a woman on crutches out of the lift. She buzzed on the door to a ward and disappeared into it. Then Flambeau and Postman were alone. Flambeau looked up at his friend: he could see that Postman was at a loss, but he couldn't help asking, '*And now?*'

'*What name would she have used?*' asked Postman in return.

Flambeau shook his head. '*I don't know.*'

Now each was as lost as the other.

A cleaning lady with a loaded trolley swaggered into the hallway like a slow-moving sea vessel. Flambeau and Postman could tell she was African and they nodded a greeting. The boy hoped wildly that she would set them on the correct course and towards that end he greeted her with a respectful, '*Good morning, mother.*'

She pointedly ignored him, stopped her trolley at the far end of the hall and pulled a tin of snuff out of her pocket. She took a pinch between her fingers then held it to her nose and sniffed. Finally she answered him, in English, 'Who is your mama, boy?'

Her hostile gaze drove Flambeau's eyes down to his feet.

'Her name is Bijou and the boy is looking for her,' said Postman. 'That's why we are here.'

The cleaning lady spat. 'Are you not looking for the watches and rings lying next to the sick people's beds?'

Flambeau was astonished by her question. He looked at her and then at Postman. Postman looked away and laughed.

'You think I'm funny? That is good,' said the cleaning lady, and she sniffed a second pinch of snuff into her other nostril.

Flambeau and Postman watched the ensuing sneeze gather force. When it finally arrived the reflex seemed to propel her to the door. She glanced back as she left and said, 'I know your kind.'

She was right. Postman was a consummate thief. He leant against the wall in the stillness that followed her departure and said, '*Need a watch?*' He said it because he could see Flambeau needed something to take his mind off things.

Flambeau looked at him aghast. Postman looked at his feet. '*Old habit.*'

They were silent for a moment.

'*It kept us alive.*' Postman said to Flambeau. And it did. As children, he and Knight had fleeced the drunk and mournful patrons of the open-air bars overlooking the stinking Ndjili streets. Postman and Knight had grown cocky as their successes mounted.

Ndjili was a wild place. And utterly lawless. The people there took it upon themselves to police their own streets and they did it with a devastating cruelty.

'Did you ever get caught?' whispered Flambeau, breathless.

'I did,' said Postman, '*Eish!* I thought that day was the end for me.'

The lowlife in the corner of the bar had let Postman fumble for his money just long enough to get a good grip on the boy's wrist.

He grabbed him so hard and held on so tight that the child's fingertips swelled up as if they had been stung by a swarm of bees.

The first blow was hard enough to split the skin on the side of Postman's head.

Knight heard his cries and tried to reach him, but the throng was thick and had no patience with yet another light-fingered urchin.

Through the forest of their legs Knight could see the blows rain down on Postman's body.

They left him in the road with five broken ribs, a cracked jaw, eyes swollen shut and skin torn from his back where they had dragged him over the rough ground.

Knight tried to pick him up, but even then Postman was a thickset boy and his dead weight brought Knight to his knees.

That's when he saw the shopping trolley lying on its side in the ditch. The front had fallen out and one wheel had lost its rubber rim and so dragged in a contradictory direction. But to Knight, it was a lifesaver.

With the help of a passing drunk, Knight lifted his friend's broken body into the trolley and pushed it along the gutted road to where the tar surface began.

He talked to Postman the whole way to the clinic, told him jokes and sang him songs. Later Postman told him it was the sound of

'Save the Last Dance For Me' that pulled him back from the brink.

Whenever Postman's eyes fell closed the young Knight sang them open again. He sang the Joseph Kabasele version, in French, set to a Congo Rhumba beat. '*So darlin; save the last dance for me . . .*'

The doctor was a kind man, tired and prematurely old. He admitted Postman, bound his broken ribs and tied up his jaw. He dressed his skinless back, stitched up his cuts and gashes and then gave him morphine.

He let Knight sleep on the floor beside Postman's bed that night. He didn't have to tell him that all the other patients in the clinic had HIV/AIDS. Knight knew what he was looking at. The doctor said at least Postman didn't have that.

'*It wasn't a shopping trolley,*' murmured Flambeau to Postman in the empty hallway of the hospital. '*It was a chariot.*'

They were quiet for a long time after he said that.

The dark shape of the cleaning lady with a security guard at her side loomed on the far side of the double doors.

Postman's instinct for trouble saw their approach a second before they breached the doors. '*Go. Go. Now!*' he hissed to Flambeau.

And they ran for the stairs.

They passed a skeletal young woman smoking a fag on the steps.

Further down, an old lady in a pink dressing gown smiled up at Postman as if she knew him, and called out, 'Oh, just a minute, love. Please . . .'

But they didn't wait. As they arrived at the entrance to the lobby Postman said, 'Slow down. Walk. Just walk.'

And he whistled under his breath as they ambled across the hospital lobby bustling with security guards and nurses.

They stepped out onto the street.

And then Flambeau ran. Not in a straight line as he would when chased, but in a circle around Postman to show his relief.

It didn't take the child long to realise that what felt like a victory just then was really a defeat. The truth was they were no closer to finding Bijou than they had been that morning, and although Postman had unveiled a fine instinct for seeing trouble coming, his talents as a sleuth had been much less certain.

By the time they reached the end of the long walk home both Flambeau and Postman had fallen into a melancholy silence.

# Sapeur

It was raining hard the day Knight arrived at the flat with a bag of Royal Mail over his shoulder. He looked like Father Christmas. Eleanor shook her head in disbelief. 'Where in the name of God and the angels did you get that?' she asked.

Knight didn't answer. 'Well?' she asked again as if in answer to her question. Postman followed his friend into the room and mischievous laughter rose up in the two men like the steam in a kettle. They were off – shrill as a couple of schoolgirls. Knight lay in the top notes, high and full of intoxicating joy. Postman added the percussion, '*ts-ts-ts*', which grounded it all underneath. Together, it was a kind of music.

Eleanor sighed. 'Look and learn from the grown-ups, Flambeau.'

The boy leaned against the doorframe and smiled. He had heard that laughter before. It was how he and Pelo sounded when they had survived the deadly gas of Lake Kivu.

Postman tried to staunch his laughter. 'Sorry.'

'Oh Good Lord,' said Eleanor, but she couldn't help smiling too.

When he caught his breath, Postman said, 'You are looking at a *good man*, my sister.'

'How is that?' asked Eleanor.

'I took on ALL of my friend Pete's work,' said Postman, 'so that he could go and see the ladyfriend who has stolen his heart.'

Knight emptied the bag onto the floor with a flourish.

'And this is how you plan to deliver it?' asked Eleanor.

'*Ey, ey, eish!*' said Postman, as he gyrated his rear end. 'Oh Pete loves that girl.'

Both men laughed.

Poor Pete. Eleanor knew he didn't stand a chance against this gangster from Ndjili who could spin a tale like no other. She could bet that just this minute the Englishman was realising that he had lost his job. He was probably retching into the toilet of his local pub and wishing he had never laid eyes on the Congolese charmer.

Postman shook his head and sighed, laughter trailing away. 'Ah Pete. What can he do?' He pulled off his jacket and sat down at the table. '*But Deo will skin us for cutting him out.*' He looked at Knight as he spoke and a shadow fell across his face.

'*He won't know,*' said Knight, as he ripped open an envelope.

'*Let's hope,*' murmured Postman.

Knight looked up sharply and hissed, '*He won't know, brother. Right?*'

Their eyes locked for a moment, and then Postman looked away and nodded.

Flambeau wondered how the grown-ups could be laughing like a couple of mad hyenas one minute and as silent as the newly dead the next.

Postman spotted the official brown of a government envelope at the bottom of the pile of post and reached for it. He smiled as he read out the words, '*Student grant cheque. Sylvia Harrison.*' He and Knight grinned at one another.

Knight shook his head in mock sympathy. '*Poor Sylvia.*' He took the cheque, examined it and handed it on to Eleanor.

'My name's not Sylvia,' she said quietly.

It was not the first time he had asked her to impersonate someone to abet his fraud. Eleanor didn't ever ask how you could change a few letters on a cheque and make it yours. Or how someone could forge a driving licence, or indeed how ordinary people could send something in the post with stamps on it and have it end up on her living-room floor. Maybe it was because she was just nineteen, but she never thought of it as criminal. But it was. And so was he. And so was she.

Her pa would have turned in his grave if he could have seen her.

She cocked her head, just long enough to make Knight sweat, and then she took the cheque and said, 'I suppose it beats being an Eleanor.'

Knight smiled with relief and kissed her forehead.

She bit the inside of her mouth. Whenever the famine of their economic universe was swept away by a coming feast, it took Eleanor a few minutes to get over her frugal nature and embrace it.

That didn't mean she didn't like the money. She realised she couldn't do a thing without it. Not pay the rent, for starters, and certainly not go to Rome or Budapest. But, honestly, she would have preferred not to bring Sylvia Harrison into it.

Knight pulled another cheque out of the pile, opened it and read the name, 'David Odibayo. Child benefit . . . backdated . . . June 08.' He and Postman both whistled.

Then Knight looked at Flambeau and said, 'I need a son.'

Flambeau glanced up from his position in the doorway.

Knight smiled at him. '*Okay with you?*'

Eleanor couldn't bear the open longing on the boy's face.

Flambeau hesitated a moment then stretched his tie and snapped it back against his neck. He grinned and said, 'Okay.'

The day Knight came home with a forged driving licence in Sylvia's name Eleanor knew they were in business.

She dressed carefully for her mission, then she sat in the bedroom in the dark. She needed a moment to prepare.

She went to the post office ahead of the boys. She handed over the cheque and driver's licence. She was halfway through stuffing Sylvia's money into her wallet when Knight and Flambeau came in.

They were the picture of easy prosperity – an elegant businessman and his beautiful son. Their glamour seemed to rattle the post office attendant, as if it were too good to be true. He looked at the cheque and said, 'I need to get authorisation on this amount, Mr Odibayo.'

Knight kept his cool. 'Please.'

The post office worker shuffled off. Flambeau looked up at Knight. '*What he call you?*'

'Sshh.' Knight put his hand on the boy's shoulder.

The post office manager's face peered at Knight through the glass cubicle beyond.

The worker returned and began silently to stuff Knight's leather bag with fifty-pound notes until Flambeau's eyes were out on stalks.

Neither Eleanor nor Flambeau had ever seen a building of such pink and lavish plenty as Harrods department store. They stood in front of its stone façade and gaped until Knight laughed and pulled them inside.

The Egyptian escalator was dazzling. Knight sailed up it like a movie star. Flambeau paused at the door to pre-teen fashion. A jewellery stand caught his eye. He tentatively selected a gaudy glass-and-pearl necklace. '*For Mama.*'

'*Mais oui.*'

Flambeau was beginning to enjoy himself. He was like one of those people you saw on television having the time of their life except *they* didn't have a morose security guard eyeing them from the door.

Flambeau moved between the rows of clothes and it felt a bit like walking through a field of cassava the way they brushed past his face. He even heard the wind rushing through leaves.

At the other end of the row stood a redheaded boy, dressed with the ease of the very wealthy. His mother and father flanked him, supremely at home here.

Flambeau stopped in his tracks. He could see they disapproved of him so completely that their disdain sucked the air out of his lungs.

Knight tried to guide him past them, but the child slipped into the row of shirts and shook his head. '*I want to go home.*'

Knight knew what the boy was feeling.

He crouched beside him and spoke softly in their shared language. '*What? You just a piece of rubbish from Bukavu, with no business being here?*'

Flambeau looked at him. His friend had named his feeling precisely. That in itself was miraculous. He nodded.

Knight was having none of that. '*Mais non. You are Flambeau. Le Sapeur congolais.*'

Knight reached for the sleeve of a shirt on the rail. '*You have Gaultier on your back.*' He grabbed a pair of trousers. '*And Ralph Lauren on your legs. You have Yamomoto on your feet and Versace on your top. You have the fashion kings of America and Italy, England and Japan in your corner. And you will wear them better than anyone.*'

Knight's words were like rain on a parched desert. '*You are Flambeau, after all.*'

And Flambeau glowed.

Knight held out his hand. '*Come.*'

Flambeau stepped out of the row of clothes and a great gust of wind entered with him. The redheaded boy and his bunch of grotesques disappeared in the sudden squall and in their stead stood Flambeau dressed head to toe in designer gear. Shining.

Knight hung a sizzling gold chain and pendant around his neck and said, '*Now you are ready.*'

# Feast

Eleanor could tell that Knight was going to pull out all the stops for the boy. Her ma would have put the money in the bank and died with it still sitting there. Her dad would have drunk it away. But the three of them, that day, were going to BE it.

Knight's shiny blue car sailed like a boat down the gracious streets of Knightsbridge. Its automatic roof peeled back to reveal the three of them alight within.

Eleanor had an enormous pink suitcase on wheels on the seat beside her, courtesy of Sylvia Harrison. She was planning on using it for her travels with Knight.

He leaned over and loosened her ponytail. Her hair fell around her face. She didn't look half bad. 'Ta,' she said, and he kissed her. Things were so good when life gave them a little break.

Flambeau and Eleanor worked their way through a small mountain of cakes and sandwiches, one after the other, methodically and seriously.

Her favourite was the creamy-brown meringue with the sweet truffle inside. His was the scones and cream. Even if you are Scottish, it is a rush to be rich on someone else's money.

Their feast was punctuated now and then by a bell that the manager of the tea salon used to call his staff. It sounded like the bell in the falling-down hotel in Kinlochbervie, which you hit when you wanted Jimmy the barman to slope out of the kitchen and serve you a beer.

*Ping!* And then again. *Ting!*

Then it came again in a run of three, *ting-ting-ting!* and Flambeau was on his feet. Moving like a boxer, a jab to the right and one to the left, he swung a punch at an invisible foe and then one more. Yes! He's down.

Eleanor wanted to cry as she laughed because she realised she'd never seen the child happy. It was a beautiful sight. He reduced the old lady in the corner to helpless laughter. Even the urbane Arab gentleman a few tables away let out a guffaw.

Flambeau danced around the table punching this way and that and when the *ping!* sounded once more he turned to face the imaginary crowd and held his hands up, victorious. The whole room clapped.

Knight leaned back in his chair and considered the boy until the scattered applause had died away. Then he asked quietly, '*Did they say your mama lived at Broadwater Farm? Or just went there to dance?*'

Flambeau said, '*There was no dancing when I was there.*'

'*What day did you go?*'

Flambeau shrugged. '*Don't know.*'

'*A weekday?*'

The child nodded. Knight laughed, ruffled his hair. '*The dancing is only at weekends.*'

Flambeau went very still. '*Like today?*'

In the silence that followed Eleanor said, 'I could always speak Gaelic. See how you two liked it.'

But Flambeau didn't even hear her. The question of his mother settled on him like a vengeful ghost. He locked his gaze on Knight and said, *'Tomorrow?'*

*'Slow down, boy.'* But it was too late for that. He was a hunter, after all.

Flambeau pushed Knight's hand away. His face was deadly serious. *'Now?'*

Not even Knight could stare down the determination in those young eyes.

# Le Pitch

It was as if a shadow had entered the vehicle with them as they drove to the housing estate. No one spoke.

When they pulled up in Knight's blue car, the only thing they could see was a lone child kicking a football against a distant wall in an otherwise deserted quadrangle.

Eleanor clutched her suitcase and scooted across the seat towards the door. Flambeau started to follow her, when Knight put his hand on the child's arm to stop him. She saw him do it, but pretended to herself that it had no meaning.

Eleanor struggled out of the car with her suitcase and then turned to wait for the others.

But no one got out. Knight leaned over to pull the door closed without looking at her.

'Hey!' she said.

The car moved off slowly. 'Hey. Wait,' said Eleanor. But they didn't wait. Neither of their two round heads, one tall and one small, turned to look at her.

When they sped away she shouted out, uselessly, 'Fuck you, Knight. Fuck you.'

★

Eleanor dragged her pink suitcase up the dirty stairwell, thump, thump, thump. Then she saw Laetitia in the deserted courtyard below.

The older woman was struggling to salvage a discarded sofa from the skip in the corner. Pretty bloody lonely task, pulling this piece of furniture out of the skip and across the vast quadrangle.

Eleanor watched her labour. The young woman's heart felt as if it had remained in the car with the boys and that the further away they went from her the closer it came to fraying, to ripping, to snapping.

Knight's blue car bumped over the grass towards the football pitch. The line of people waiting to get in the gate all turned to see who was arriving. Knight. Yes. Everyone knew him. Flambeau followed. When he saw where he was, he reached for Knight's hand in gratitude.

Le Pitch was bursting with life. Each woman's face had the real possibility of being his mama. Every back-of-head. It was like seeing after being blind.

Flambeau was dazzled by the wide-mouthed laugh of the pretty woman in the trilby hat and the pout of her less lovely friend.

He wondered at the flower painted on the cheek of the teenager in the shiny gold shirt. He saw how furtively the tall, skinny boy watched the women on the dance floor.

Flambeau saw every kind of feeling on every kind of face. But none was his mother. And so he turned away.

Knight stopped beside him and said, '*She's not here.*'

'*She's not here today, but she might be here tomorrow,*' said Flambeau.

Knight offered the boy his hand and said, '*But you are here now.*'

Flambeau nodded.

'*And for what do people come here?*' asked Knight.

'*To see each other,*' said Flambeau.

'*And?*' prompted Knight.

'*To eat good pondu,*' said Flambeau with a shrug.

'*And?*'

'*To remember the Congo?*' murmured Flambeau, uncertain.

Knight shook his head and said, '*To forget.*'

And then he said more quietly, '*To forget the things they can do nothing about.*'

Flambeau looked across at the dance floor. A small sea of forgetting was going on there for sure.

Knight smiled at Flambeau and offered his arm. '*And to dance.*'

Flambeau hesitated a moment too long and Knight swept onto the dance floor without him. Flambeau cursed himself. He had missed his chance.

Flambeau watched Knight hungrily as he danced across the floor: cool, sexy, commanding – the prince of princes. He glided through the dancers and everywhere he went he brought smiles to people's faces. Flambeau needed some of that. It was irresistible.

At first the boy was unable to move a muscle in spite of having made the journey from the edge to the centre of the dance floor. Then a smiling woman took his small hand in hers and began to draw him out. Pretty soon the music had him moving. The beat was so much his own. His Rhumba. And even though his mother was not there to share the moment, he allowed it to draw him in and then occupy him totally.

Flambeau didn't see when Knight stopped dancing. Neither did he see the cause. If he had, he would have saved himself a lot of time and maybe things would have turned out very differently. But he didn't.

It was Manu the Trafficker, with his dark hat and skeletal face, who drew Knight out of the dancing.

Knight leant against the wall beside him, but did not greet him.

Manu was the first to speak. '*Got nothing for you today, homeboy.*'

'*I don't want anything you can give me,*' said Knight.

Manu's response was to spit onto the dust at Knight's feet.

The air between them prickled with animosity, but neither chose to push it into direct conflict. They waited.

Out of the corner of his eye Knight saw Manu pick out Flambeau amongst the dancers and watch him with particular interest. It brought a chill of disquiet into Knight's bones.

Knight murmured, '*You know him?*'

'*Who?*' said Manu.

'*You know that child?*'

Manu feigned ignorance. '*What child?*'

The boy was in the heart of the dancers. He was moving like a dervish.

Knight asked again, '*You know Flambeau?*'

He got no answer. Something in his body churned with alarm. Could this be the boy's trafficker? Knight pushed his hands deep into his pockets to calm himself. What a cruel web of association it would reveal if it were so.

If Eleanor had asked that same question he would have admonished her: *Ah, mais non, chérie, that will make you crazy, that question.* And so it would. Knight shrugged it off. He said nothing when he felt Manu the Trafficker push himself away from the wall and move away through the crowds.

The child was lost in the DJ's whooping loud Kinshasa beat. The woman on the stage did her jaw-dropping gyration. The sun was setting. Flambeau was home. He was happy and he was home.

Knight swallowed his vestigial unease and slipped back into the dancing crowd.

When the other woman first arrived on the dance floor Flambeau was as dazzled as everyone else by her beauty and her sass.

Knight danced towards her with edgy abandon. She attached herself to him with an ease that suggested she had done so many times before. She danced sexy, against Knight's body. Flambeau's eyes widened with surprise at her lasciviousness.

Knight waited until Flambeau's back was turned before he led the woman off the dance floor. The boy saw it anyway. She was wrapped so tight around Knight it was clear, even to the child, what they were going for.

Knight turned to look at Flambeau as he went. Put his finger to his lips.

A moment, and then the boy nodded his collusion.

# Shoes

Flambeau put one foot in front of the other as he left Le Pitch, just as he always did when he walked, but his feet didn't feel the same. He looked down at them. It struck him that his shoes looked like something a vagrant would wear and he chided himself silently for their disrepair. What kind of Sapeur would be seen dead in shoes like that? Moulded to someone else's foot, too wide, too crude, too ugly.

He hated those shoes. They made his feet hot. As he walked his anger grew. They were downright unworthy.

He would not have been able to say it in words, but so was he. It was shame that made the sweat pool between his toes. He had transgressed. He had proved his loyalty to Knight and his lies and so had betrayed Eleanor.

Ah, the heat.

Flambeau crouched down to tear off his shoes, but the laces were so knotted that freeing his feet was a slow and laborious process.

He needed the roof and the birds to calm his raucous self-loathing. He needed his mother to tell him that his betrayal stopped short of that committed by the mad Scottish king she had told him about as they hid under the sink.

He abandoned the task of untying his shoes and ran. If he had known where he was, he would have flown home, but he didn't and so he darted right and then left, he hit into walls and was caught briefly in a cul-de-sac.

From above, his passage looked like a panicked bird battering itself to bits on the wire walls of its cage.

It was only when he spotted the high red-brick walls of the hospital that Flambeau slowed down and got his bearings.

He did not look up or wonder about anything in his path until he had crossed the housing estate, climbed the stairs and pushed open the red door to his sanctuary.

Then he stopped.

Eleanor's hair was tied up in a rag and she was on her knees in the birdcage surrounded by bird shit. Her presence there was so unexpected and her task so abject that it took him a moment before he could think, let alone speak.

It only added to his shame that the first thought that struck him was that, today at least, *Eleanor was a dishrag.*

He approached the birdcage tentatively. He feared that she might smell the betrayal on his skin. Or that she might rant and rave about being left behind. But all she did was smile at him and wipe a loose hair from her forehead. Her fight was not with him.

She knew Knight was going to wait until her humiliation had faded and the bare-skinned hunger underneath had driven her to near despair. Then he would take her in his arms and she would weep with gratitude.

He always waited for that.


Flambeau climbed into the birdcage to help her clean it out and found a packet tucked under the box he always sat on.

It was an H&M packet, and in it was a pair of school shoes. He wondered for a moment how he had become a lucky person. Someone who longed for something and then, moments later, had the object of his longing appear. He didn't linger with that thought, but tore open the bunched-up laces of the old shoes and carefully tied the laces on the new. He stretched his toes into the plentiful space at the tip of the shoes and sighed. It was luxury, that space. Luck and luxury. He stood up.

Eleanor looked at him. His shorts and skinny legs with shoes like ships made her heart lurch. 'From your aunt?' she asked softly.

Flambeau nodded.

Flambeau tried a few steps of the Rhumba in his new shoes. He did a little sidestep or two and clapped his hands. That was when Eleanor stood up and said, 'Come on. Right here. Right now.'

'What?'

She climbed out of the cage. 'I want to learn more of that . . . that . . .'

'The Rhumba?'

'That's the one.'

She stood with her arms open in anticipation. He stepped reluctantly into her embrace and they began to dance.

She was hopeless. He was great. The birds clustered on the wire as if looking on.

He endured it as long as he could.

She looked at him and said, 'That's it?'

He nodded.

'Not much to it,' she said, her disappointment making her cruel.

'If you saw them at Le Pitch you wouldn't say that,' he snapped.

'Le what?'

He looked at her. Stricken. He knew he had made a mistake. He muttered, 'Nothing.'

'Flambeau?'

He looked up at her.

'Was that where Knight took you today?'

He vowed silently to himself that he would cut out his tongue next time he had the chance.

'Flambeau?'

This time he didn't look up. But he nodded. It was Le Pitch.

Eleanor spoke simple and soft. 'Why didn't he take me there?'

There it was again, the impossible question. Flambeau looked at her. This time the other woman filled in all the answers, sucked all the reason and nuance out of his prior deliberations. What could he say?

She looked up at the clouds as they passed overhead. She was achingly sad. The terrible truth for that young boy was that his silence only added to it.

# Killing Me Softly

On weekend nights the minicab office was fed by a steady stream of Londoners in pursuit of diversion. The young ones stumbled in with eyes dilated with drink or drugs, or simply by the precarious business of seeking pleasure in a city so full of the desperate and the lost. They came to be saved and driven home to safer climes. Or they came hunting for more, as if to say, *Show me, show me those who know something that I do not.*

The older ones were often tired, silent spouses by their sides. Disappointment hung about them, as if wherever they had been had not quite lived up to its transformative promise. Then there were those, rank with fear and dripping blood, who needed a hospital *right bloody now*.

All these and more washed in and then out again with drivers in tow. It was Friday night after all, and there was a whole week of London living to obliterate.

It was difficult to sleep alongside the minicab office when it was busy like this, but Postman somehow managed it.

He rolled a towel out on the carpet and covered himself with a blanket. In the mornings he washed at the small sink in the office toilet. He wasn't familiar with beds and houses and families.

This worked for him.

On the odd occasion when both Postman and Knight slept in the office, Knight got the floor and Postman toughed it out in the chair. That was how it was tonight.

Knight was in the deepest of sleeps when his phone rang to the tune of 'Killing Me Softly'. It raised both Knight and Postman from their slumber with a gasp.

Knight put the phone to his ear and murmured, '*Oui.*' What he heard did not please him. He said simply, '*Where do I go?*'

He listened and then he hung up. He pulled the blanket over his head and rocked his body to and fro. Postman watched him for a moment and then he said, 'Deo?'

Knight didn't answer. He rocked.

Knight could still picture the miracle of how Deo looked the very first time he saw him.

Word on the street that day was that there was going to be a *challenge* in Kinshasa's biggest outdoor *nganda* between two high-ranking Sapeurs. They were fighting over a woman.

Knight and Postman may have been only eleven and thirteen at the time but they sniffed out the *nganda* as desert animals find water. They found a good vantage point through the fence.

At the very pinnacle of the rite, when the two Sapeurs delivered their final shots of sartorial mastery and the crowds roared their support of one or the other, just at that moment, the two boys heard a voice behind them. '*You want to look like them?*'

Knight and Postman turned to see a man so beautifully dressed that they believed he must be a king. Pink shirt, pink shoes and shiny black trousers. It was Deo. '*You want what they have? These Sapeurs?*' he said.

Knight was on his feet. '*Oui, monsieur.*'

Postman was more cautious, but only marginally so. '*You can teach us the ways of La Sape?*'

'*Mais oui.*' Deo stood up and held out a hand for each child. The two street children gratefully accepted Deo's outstretched hands.

The three of them began to weave their way through the dazzling crowds. The children could not believe their luck. For once, they were blessed.

If only he and Postman had run while they still had a chance.

As Deo led them through the crowds towards their glowing future, the two children did not notice the frayed cuffs on his shirt or the way his shoes were tied with string. The truth was that their beautifully dressed seducer was poverty-stricken and they were part of his plan to change all that.

Deo was as green to the business of kidnapping and trafficking children as they were to the world outside Ndjili. It made him more hazardous by far.

They all three slept that night in the bus shelter. Deo tied string around each of their ankles to stop them running away then fell asleep on the bench. Knight and Postman did not speak or look at one another but huddled close until the sun came up.

For years afterwards they wondered why they didn't just bite through the string with their teeth. It would have saved so much suffering.

Postman followed Knight out of the minicab office and onto the street. They were locked in a conversation so intense they were oblivious to all else.

Knight opened his car door and Postman said, '*I'm telling you. Don't go.*'

Knight turned to him and hissed, '*Do I have a choice?*'

Postman ran his fingers across his head. '*Maybe he knows?*'

'*What?*'

'*About the cheques.*'

Knight shook his head. '*He's punishing me for the mosque. For delivering Fatima late. Or not delivering her. Or whatever the fuck it was.*'

Postman looked at him and whispered, '*Then you won't come back.*'

Knight looked at his friend. '*I'll come back.*'

Postman shook his head.

Knight saw his grave face and spoke more softly. '*We've made it this far, brother. Right?*' Knight smiled, a poor attempt at an everything-will-be-okay smile.

'*Go home to Eleanor and the boy*,' Postman hissed in bullet-swift patois. '*They are waiting.*'

It got Knight's attention because this was the language that had evolved in their slum and come of age in their shared suffering and mutual shame.

*Not home. Not yet.* Knight closed his eyes and leant his head on the car door.

Postman changed tack, his face taking on a fleeting joy. '*We could go somewhere else. To Russia . . . or Mexico.*'

Knight didn't even lift his head up when he said, 'Don't be stupid.'

He said it in English, and the words shut down all hope. That's when Postman knew he had failed. He brushed his hand over Knight's bowed head and walked back into the minicab office, the curve of his back like that of a much older man.

★

Knight drove through mile after mile of dark, wet streets. He turned into a disused scrap yard. Anthills of old tyres rose up, haphazard in the wasteland around the crumbling warehouse.

The door to the low building was manned by two Congolese bouncers, but the easy authority usually attending such figures was absent. They were jumpy, on their toes. One of the bouncers shone a powerful torch at Knight as he got out of the car. When he saw who it was he called out in Ndjili slang, '*Hey, brother.*'

Knight nodded his head, but did not speak. He moved slowly. His dark suit and white shirt looked more subdued professional than Sapeur.

The bouncers wordlessly opened the door for Knight. A roar of noise surged out into the night as they did so.

Knight paused in the doorway when he heard the baying sound, his face inscrutable, then he stepped inside. If he had been his own man, Knight would have obeyed his instincts and quietly taken his leave the moment he smelt the blood and fear in the air. But he was not.

He saw a thick knot of men gathered under the grotesquely bright light suspended from the ceiling. It deepened the shadows around it and robbed those in its rays of all colour.

It was from those dark shadows that Knight chose his vantage point. From there he could see the two men locked in combat on the makeshift platform.

They looked like one creature, the head of one held in a low vice grip by the arms of the other. From a distance they looked quite still. As if they had fallen unexpectedly into an embrace. It was almost peaceful.

Knight knew better. As he moved closer he could see the strain in every muscle as each fighter tried to push the other off balance. A single roar full of grit and desperation gave one of the fighters the force to break free. He began to lift his arms to celebrate his liberation, but his opponent took him around the neck and pounded thud, thud, thud, at his ribs. His face darkened as the air was pushed out of his shrinking lungs.

Knight saw Deo watching the fighters from the front row. He saw him rise to his feet and shout at the trapped fighter, '*Come now. Push him off! Come on.*'

It wasn't often that Knight could observe Deo without being seen. The older man's elegance was even more seamless than usual – pale pink leather shoes with a matching tie and all the rest a silky black. It was a sight almost as miraculous as the first time he had seen him.

Deo's man in the ring began to spit foam and shake. Knight watched his heavy body slip to the floor like a plastic balloon full of viscous liquid.

'*Non!*' Deo rose up to his full height and shouted. 'No.' It was as if he expected the comatose man to crawl to his feet at that command. But of course he didn't. It seemed to devastate Deo.

On the other side of the ring, a tall man in a long fur coat rose to his feet baying victory. He stepped onto the platform and held up the arm of his fighter.

Deo turned away. The man in the fur coat shouted above the crowd, '*Again, Deo?*'

Deo stopped. The man called out once more, '*Come, brother. Another round.*'

Deo considered this challenge. He raised his head and in the brutal overhead light Knight saw that he was ancient, his face lined and grey as if cut from coal. Deo had been shamed.

For years Knight had watched Deo and his cronies transform the nonviolent *challenges* between Sapeurs into fight clubs with a money prize. Deo was the first to offer up his 'boys' as gladiators. It was those who had displeased Deo who had the most to fear. He would send them out into the crowd. They would wait there and watch, adrenalin racing through their veins, for the nod of Deo's head which meant it was their turn.

Tonight was no different. A quick glance around the room told Knight that apart from the poor soul in the ring, he was the only one of Deo's boys here. He broke into a sweat. He wanted to go home to his family. He froze. He had thought of Eleanor as 'his' for a long time but this was the first moment that word, *family*, conjured itself. It sent a silent prayer, unbidden and unconscious, to his lips.

Knight hadn't prayed for a long time. His mother had taken him to church every Sunday in the lean-to on the edge of Ndjili where the people swayed and sang and shouted out noisy, beseeching prayers. Loud enough to make sure that God and everyone else heard their fealty.

It was a Catholic church, or rather the mixture of Catholic doctrine and ancestral worship that rendered it all utterly terrifying to the young Knight. Even though there was one all-powerful God, he was joined by numerous ancestral adjutants, all ready and waiting to find the sin in him and to punish it. All of them had to be assuaged.

If there were a God, how could he let his mother be so ravaged and this cruel pretender, Deo, step in to take her place?

Deo looked around the room at the faces in the crowd. Knight knew he was looking for him but he did not step out of the shadows. Maybe this time he wouldn't. Maybe he would flee with Eleanor and

Flambeau as Postman had suggested? A fresh start. He wished momentarily that he believed in such things.

Deo turned to the chanting crowd and shouted out, '*My boy, he didn't come.*' He didn't say this to anyone in particular. Just out into the night. '*My best boy.*'

The crowd roared at his helplessness, merciless, insistent.

Knight moved slowly out of the shadows.

Deo did not see Knight's slow approach towards the ring. In his desperation the older man took his phone out of his pocket and dialled a number, hunched over like a tramp.

As Knight stepped onto the far side of the platform the phone in his pocket began to ring.

Amongst the raging laughter and derision all around him, Deo picked out the distant strains of 'Killing Me Softly' . . . and his face lit up.

Knight took his phone out of his pocket and held it high as he made his way into the ring. '*Killing me softly . . .*'

He looked at Deo only once. A baffling glance of what looked from the outside like mutual love and devotion passed between them. But it was not love, it was the putrid intimacy of slave and master. It was the kind of look that binds one, fatally, to the other.

# Home

The first blow hit Knight's cheek with such force that a spray of spit and blood arched up into the air above the fighters.

Deo watched its passage with surprise. A single drop of sweat ran from his hairline into his mouth.

Knight recovered and turned to take in his foe. He could see that his opponent was new to London. He had the sinewy arms and desperate eyes of a recent arrival. From eastern Congo maybe? A soldier? His body suggested that. He was hungry for victory because he had nothing else.

Knight had been like that once. It was no longer so. Now he trawled his body and his will for the fight he knew this required and he came away empty-handed. Flambeau and Eleanor's love had shifted him into a softer world and it equipped him not at all for what he was now facing.

At the second blow Deo closed his eyes.

Knight blinked in surprise as the feeling tore through his ribs. The sound of bone snapping marked the beginning of his defeat, but he knew he would have to endure much before the end.

The blows rained down but they brought the crowd no joy. It was a rout, dispirited and inevitable. They knew the crushing blow to

Knight's kidneys and the spurt of blood from his mouth that followed meant he had been vanquished.

Deo got to his feet but this time he did not shout encouragement or implore his fighter.

He simply turned and walked out.

Knight saw only a fleeting glimpse of Deo leaving as he fell. He called out, but the sound stuck in his devastated throat. Deo did not look back.

It took a long time for Knight to open his eyes again. By then the warehouse was deserted and the parking lot empty of cars. It was as if no one had ever been there.

Knight's long, slow, one-handed drive through the streets of London left him utterly spent. He sat in his car for an hour before he could muster the strength to climb the stairs of the housing estate. But he did. He was wounded and he needed home.

He stood beside Eleanor's bed for a long time and watched the in and out of her breath. Somewhere in that quiet vigil she became aware of him. She didn't wonder why he stood over her doing nothing in the dead of night. She did not speak or even open her eyes. She waited.

She felt him lift the covers and slip as quietly as he could into the bed. She lay still and maintained her steady breathing so she could savour the care he took not to wake her.

He crept close and he breathed her in. He closed his eyes and rested there.

She turned around. Their two faces on the pillow were still. She wary. He ruined. She ran her finger across his cheek and he moaned. He turned his head to kiss her and she saw the long sliver of a cut behind his ear.

'What is this?' she asked.

'It is nothing.' He tried to keep her focused on his eyes.

'It is not nothing.' Eleanor opened her mouth to ask more but he put his fingers on her lips and then he said, 'I lost.'

Eleanor lifted the sheets away from their two bodies. She could see from the way he lay that he was hurt. She unbuttoned his shirt and gently pulled it off his one arm, then his other, then his back. The bruises and scrapes of rough combat marked him like a map. Knight sat up with enormous effort. His face was swollen on the one side, a dark, slick bruise was spreading over his chest. He looked at her.

Eleanor felt the inky pall of fear rise up in her body and she whispered, 'What happened to you?'

He touched her cheek and murmured, 'Congo.'

She washed him with a warm cloth. He allowed her to lift his limbs and wipe them clean until his battered body lay still and glistening like a seal. He then took her hand and whispered, '*Chérie*.'

Their bodies were so closely wound up together the following morning that Flambeau couldn't bring himself to wake them.

Postman arrived not long after, grave with worry. 'He okay?' he asked when he saw Eleanor in the doorway.

'He's alive.'

'You?'

'I don't know.' Eleanor made him a cup of tea and he thanked her. Flambeau got to work on the salt fish he knew Knight would want for breakfast.

When Knight walked into the living room a short time later he moved like an old man.

Postman stood up. He opened his arms and Knight stepped inside his embrace.

Eleanor and Flambeau could see how Knight rested there for a moment.

Postman murmured, '*Brother.*'

Knight said, '*I am here.*'

Then Postman handed Knight a deposit slip from a bank. Knight glanced at it and then quickly up to Postman's face. '*It's seven days.*' Postman nodded. '*It cleared yesterday. We don't have much time.*'

Postman handed Knight a fake driving licence. Knight considered it and then said, '*Help me dress.*'

Eleanor looked at Postman. 'He can't go anywhere. He's hurt.'

Knight raised the slip and said, 'This is too good to miss.'

Eleanor sat at the table and poured herself a cup of tea.

Knight looked like a million dollars when Flambeau and Postman were finished with him. He moved gingerly as he kissed Eleanor and turned to take leave of his friend.

Postman wasn't going to let that happen. '*I'm coming with you.*'

'Me too!' said Flambeau. Knight shook his head. 'No need.'

'That so?' Postman looked at Eleanor and said, 'Saving my little brother's hide . . .' he tipped his imaginary hat, '. . . is an old habit of mine.'

Knight laughed so that his ribs hurt.


Eleanor cleaned up the breakfast things after they had left for the bank. Then she went into the bathroom and prayed. She too had not done so since her early childhood. Her father had never had an ounce of faith. Her mother attended the small stone church in the village every Sunday even though the priest only came every third Sunday to perform the service.

On the days when the priest was not there, her mother huddled in the cold and grim interior and prayed fervently to be released from her choice of mate.

When Eleanor's dad fell off the roof, her mother walked to the church in the growing cold of evening and knelt down to give thanks for her deliverance.

Eleanor wished she could be delivered from Knight and his life, but it was too late for that. Much too late. She just put her head down and prayed that he would come home to her in one piece.

The two dashing men and the shining boy caused something of a stir as they walked across the great hall of the bank. They were beautiful and they were very, very foreign.

Flambeau, Knight and Postman were halfway across the gracious banking hall when Flambeau stopped walking. He didn't know why, but he had a powerful need to do that. Knight and Postman didn't seem to notice.

Flambeau saw the young Indian bank teller look at the withdrawal slip that Knight handed her and then at the driver's licence. She typed the details into the computer. What she read there startled her and she glanced up at Knight's face in alarm. She shook her head and handed both back to Knight. 'I'm sorry, sir, that account is no longer operational.'

It is possible that if Postman hadn't been there, Knight would not have been compelled to force the issue. He would have taken the licence, scooped Flambeau up and left in a dignified way. But he didn't. He handed the withdrawal slip back and insisted that she cash it.

He had learnt that insistence in the ghetto, and without it neither he nor Postman would have survived.

Flambeau dug the gold chain Knight had given him from under his shirt and held it tight. He saw Knight smile at the teller, but she was unnerved and got up to confer with a colleague seated at the desk behind her. He shook his head. Flambeau could see trouble coming.

When Knight and Postman looked at one another everything around them went quiet. There was a dare, a challenge, of such silent insistence in that glance that Flambeau's heart nearly jumped out of his chest.

Knight turned to the bank teller and in quiet but vivid African French he told her to, '*Do as I ask. Now. Please.*' And then he did the same in English only more insistently.

All the security guards and the bank tellers collectively seemed to pick something up in the air and were suddenly alert.

Postman kicked the narrow dustbin in frustration. '*Haai, haai, haai. Pay the man his money, you English.*'

It was almost an ululation, that sound, and it scared the living daylights out of everyone in the bank with its foreignness and its anger.

In the silence that followed Postman's outcry, the young Indian bank teller stood up and tapped on the pane of glass between her and Knight.

When Knight turned to look at her she said in her kindest voice, 'If you have another account you can use a cash card at the machine outside.'

Postman looked at her.

'It's outside the main doors, on the left.' The young woman moved her head minutely from side to side in a quintessentially Indian shrug. It was a philosophical gesture meant to say *This is how life is and it stinks. Sorry.* It was polite and just compassionate enough to bring them back from the brink.

Knight hung his head for a moment, then he said, 'Thank you.' And took back the slip.

He walked quickly towards Flambeau. Postman followed behind as was their ancient agreement — he was the rearguard, Knight the front man.

Knight tried the door to the bank but it did not open. He shouted, 'Open it.'

The dark shape of the manager hovered behind the glass. He wasn't going to do any such thing.

That would have been that, if the harried young mortgage adviser, back late from her lunch, hadn't punched in the code and opened the door at just that moment.

The three of them looked at her blinking face for what felt like a long time and then blasted through the gap between her small body and the open door.

# Slaves

A young red-haired girl on the pavement turned to watch Knight and Postman hurry towards the busy street with the small boy at their heels.

The gaps between the vehicles were only long enough for them to dart like lightning from one pavement to the other. The two men made no accommodation for the young Flambeau. It wasn't that kind of world.

Once across the road they hesitated, at a loss for a moment, and then Postman led them away. At first they almost expected a hand to grab them by the collar and throw them into a police van, but as the minutes passed their pace became more leisurely. Knight even stopped to catch his breath and ease the burning in his broken ribs.

Flambeau looked up at Knight's face and wondered where they were going, but he didn't ask.

They found themselves on the bank of the Thames.

That's when the phone in Knight's pocket began to ring, '*Killing me softly* . . .' Knight leant down to look at it. He held it in his palm. Then he turned it off. He simply applied a little pressure from his thumb and it was silenced.

He looked up and saw the shock on Postman's face. Knight laughed. Postman looked away.

Knight put the phone back into his pocket and led them, without stopping to buy a ticket, onto a boat full of tourists.

The three of them sat in the front of the nearly empty exterior of the boat. They were silent as they watched London's iconic buildings slip by.

Flambeau's small body was hunched over the railing, the better to see the churning current below.

Knight got up and walked to the prow of the boat. He stood there until he felt the city fall away on either side and only water lay ahead.

The silver shapes of the Thames Barrier heralded the open sea. A cormorant flew low and dark just above the surface of the waves.

Knight turned to call Flambeau and saw that the boy had come to the prow of his own accord. His face mirrored the wonder Knight felt.

It struck the older man with the force of a blow that he had been a slave to Deo for longer than Flambeau had been alive.

It was dark by the time they dropped Postman off at the office and started the long walk up the hill to the housing estate.

The pall of silent grief that had overwhelmed Knight on the boat was still evident in his face. It made him mute and deaf.

Flambeau had seen this before, especially when Knight remembered his mother. The boy recalled how Knight had tried to make him feel better in the days after Bijou had failed to arrive. He felt compelled to do the same and so as he walked he reverted to their old game. He prepared himself and then said, '*Guess. Listen and guess.*'

And then he sang in Lingala,

> *The sweetness of my mother's milk,*
> *Is far more delectable*
> *Than any food*
> *I have ever tasted.*

He smiled and glanced up at Knight. '*Come on, guess.*'
But his friend's eyes remained cast down, his limbs slow and heavy.
Flambeau nudged him with his elbow. '*You know it?*'
Knight still did not respond.
'*Come on. Try.*' Flambeau hopped impatiently by Knight's side.
He sang a little more.

> *Although you add no ingredients,*
> *It is sweeter than the sweetest sweet.*

Flambeau looked up at his friend. '*Remember? Remember that?*'
Knight walked more quickly and Flambeau fell in by his side.
They walked in silence for some time.
Then Knight began to sing, very softly.

> *The sweetness of my mother's milk,*
> *Is far more delectable*
> *Than any food*
> *I have ever tasted.*

Flambeau laughed. '*That's it!*'
Knight continued,

> *Although you add no ingredients,*
> *It is sweeter than the sweetest sweet.*

Flambeau's young voice joined in, and they sang together as they climbed the long hill, hand in hand. They evoked their continent with their song and their shared nostalgia for all things lost.

> *Since you left,*
> *I have lost my appetite.*
> *I eat now just to please my mouth.*

They reached the top of the hill and neither had the stomach to continue the song.

Flambeau turned to Knight and asked, '*Is she dead?*'

Knight turned heavily to look at him.

The boy asked again, '*Is my mama dead?*'

Knight whispered, '*I don't know.*'

Flambeau nodded, '*Me too. I don't know.*'

Knight pulled Flambeau into a hug. They remained so for a moment.

Any other time Knight would have seized the chance to boast about how he had seen Papa Wemba sing that very song at a concert his first year in London. By way of introduction, the great man had told them about his mother, the *pleureuse*, who had taught him his art by making him sing to mark the passing of the newly dead and giving comfort to those left behind.

He would have to tell Flambeau another night. Tonight was not a night for stories.

When they turned into the red-brick estate, Knight let go of Flambeau's hand and said, '*Goodnight, little man.*'

Flambeau looked at him. '*Come. Let's go home.*'

Knight shook his head.

Flambeau looked up at their brightly lit flat, then back at his friend. '*Please. She is waiting.*'

Knight shook his head. '*She is waiting for a winner.*'

Flambeau looked at him. He didn't understand.

'*She is waiting for someone with money in his pocket,*' said Knight.

Flambeau shook his head, '*She wants you.*'

'*She wants someone who can take her to Rome.*'

This brutal logic even a child could understand. Flambeau took in the defeat in Knight's face.

He asked very softly, '*Where will you go?*'

Knight lifted his finger to his lips to indicate his secret just as he had all those weeks ago at Le Pitch.

Flambeau did not nod in collusion this time. He just stood there, trying not to cry.

Knight turned away. '*Go home, Flambeau.*'

'*I want to be where you are,*' said the boy.

'*You can't.*'

'*I can. Yes, I can.*' Flambeau reached for Knight's hand.

'*Go!*' Knight hissed.

Flambeau's face crumpled and he turned and ran towards the dark and filthy steps.

# Rome

The blue light from the silent TV shifted and changed on Flambeau and Eleanor's faces. Neither spoke.

Eleanor drank the dregs of her cold tea and slipped her feet into her slippers. 'What's the time?' she asked.

Flambeau murmured, 'Don't know.'

The silence was shrill around them.

Eleanor cleared her throat. 'Did he say where he was going?'

Flambeau shook his head. He didn't dare look up.

Eleanor sighed and got to her feet. She pulled the blankets out of the cupboard to make up Flambeau's bed, but he did not get up to help her. She regarded the boy sitting on the sofa with his arms folded across his chest and she said, 'He's not coming tonight, Flambeau.'

'He might,' said the boy.

'Just go to bed,' said Eleanor.

'No,' whispered Flambeau.

She threw the blankets onto the sofa. 'Oh come on, lad.'

Flambeau pushed the blankets onto the floor and shouted, 'If I wait for him, he will come.'

'And if you sleep?' she asked.

His hands made the slightest gesture of something disappearing. Then he shrugged.

The truth was Eleanor couldn't sleep either. Her instincts were roused to the tremor of a new threat. She couldn't tell what it was, but she knew it had come.

The extremity of Knight's life was such that she had to take things at face value. He had to go when Deo called, and so he went. The question of whether he had someone else had always been there, but it lurked unformed and unspoken on the edge of her deeper fear for his safety.

Now it stepped into the light. And it was no less searing for its ordinariness.

Eleanor washed the bath and mopped the floor in the bedroom. She vacuumed the ragged curtains and then she sorted through Knight's things.

She pretended to herself that she was creating order, but deep down she knew she was really looking to discover signs of another woman.

She found nothing like that. But she did find his passport with his official picture in the front. His name, Tresor Sese Yakoko, was not printed below the photograph. It was someone else's name. She turned the pages one by one. She saw stamps for Nigeria, Belgium and England.

She wondered at how little she knew of the real journey those stamps signified. She understood only that to get to each of those destinations Knight had faced his possible end.

She came to the last page of his passport and it stopped her dead in her tracks. She sat there for a long time trying to understand it.

She got up and went into the living room. She showed Flambeau the stamp.

Flambeau looked at her and shrugged. 'What does it say?'

'It says he can't go anywhere.' She showed him the stamp again.

He squinted.

She read, 'Leave to transit for twenty-four hours.' She looked at him. 'And it is dated 1998.'

She sat down in the chair, 'He can buy me fancy shoes, but he can't step off this godforsaken island without getting sent back to the Congo forever.'

Flambeau just looked at her.

'He can't go to Rome, even for a weekend.'

The child did not say a word. He got up and walked to the front door. He stopped there and said, 'You coming?'

They lay on the netting roof of the birdcage with shared headphones in their ears.

She got it entirely now. When you don't know what to say, play the music. When you are ruffled or sad, play music. When you think you might be dead tomorrow, play music.

The cloud above them was particularly orange that night. Eleanor thought it looked like her dad's Pink Floyd record cover minus the pig in the sky. It gave her no comfort.

They lay there for a while just being company, and then she said, 'Does he have someone else?'

The boy took Eleanor's hand.

She didn't ask him again and Flambeau didn't say a word. He just held onto her hand and prayed for the question to go away.

'*Where did you get this?*' A voice barked from the shadows below them and they both jumped.

Flambeau's Aunt Laetitia was standing on the ground below them. She held out the necklace he had bought for his mother at Harrods.

Flambeau flipped his body over so he could see her better. '*I bought it at the shop. For Mama. But no one was using it so I gave it to you.*'

'*With whose money did you buy it?*' she asked.

Flambeau was silent.

'*I give you three seconds to get down here, Flambeau.*'

The boy scuttled down the wire of the cage and onto the ground.

Laetitia towered above him. '*Where did the money come from?*'

'*The post office,*' he said quietly.

She slapped his face.

'Hang on a bloody minute,' said Eleanor and she started to climb down too.

Then she saw Laetitia pull Flambeau into an embrace. His aunt held him so tight he could hardly breathe.

He spoke into the softness of her chest. '*I can't remember her face, Auntie.*'

What could she say to that? Nothing. She just put her head into the fold of his neck and breathed. They were still like that for some time.

Then Flambeau took the necklace from Laetitia, put it around her neck and did up the clasp. He considered it and then pronounced, '*Jolie.*'

As she walked past Eleanor on her way to the stairs Laetitia whispered, 'I'm watching you.'

Fair enough.

Eleanor waited until Laetitia was gone and then she turned to Flambeau and said softly, 'Want to dance?'

He shook his head. That was a step too far for him, but she had a suspicion it would comfort him to see how far she had come. 'Want to watch me?'

A slight nod.

She was useless at first. Just couldn't get the rhythm. But she tried again, *one . . . three, four, one . . . three four*, and when she did the spin, she felt it coming. Wow!

He even clapped. She did one more turn for luck. He laughed at her. She could tell he thought she looked pretty good.

She had been practising on the roof every time she could. It made her feel better. She worked on it so the top of her head got sunburnt and the muscles in her whole body began to pull tighter together.

And now she just had to ask, 'So. D'you think I'm ready?'

'For what?'

'Le Pitch.'

Oh Lord. He knew this was trouble.

'I'm going to fight for him, Flambeau.'

What could he do except feel the dread seeping up through his shoes.

The dread was still there when Flambeau opened his eyes the next morning. He leapt out of bed, disappeared into the kitchen and came back with flour on his lips.

He lay in his bed and groaned, clutching his stomach. Eleanor stumbled into his room, half asleep. She thought, for a moment, that he was dying. Then she saw the flour on his lips. It was so obvious as to be funny.

She spared him her laughter because she knew it would offend him. Instead, she folded her arms across her chest in what she hoped was a picture of disapproval and said, 'You'll have to stay in bed till we leave for Le Pitch, Flambeau, because you look like death.'

He looked at her in dismay. She disappeared into her bedroom and shouted, 'And wipe that flour off your mouth.'

Oh he was bored in that bed all morning. Out of his mind bored. He tied the sheets into elaborate knots. He stood on his head. He muttered incomprehensible things in Kinyarwanda and Lingala while she, well, she committed an act of transfiguration in her four-square bathroom.

As she worked, Eleanor began to look like someone else. She cocked her head in the mirror and wondered idly whether her mother would find it easier to love this someone else?

Eleanor never knew why her mother found it so hard. But she did. Maybe it was something in her that had broken long, long before Eleanor even came along. Maybe it was her daughter's young, everything-is-possible self that reminded her how disappointed she was with her lot. Or perhaps Eleanor just reminded her of her husband?

It was only the day after his funeral and all Eleanor's dad's worldly goods were in binliners at the back door. Her mother couldn't wait to clean him out. One bag was labelled *GIVE AWAY*, the other *FISH-ERMEN*, and then there were the boxes and boxes of books.

When Eleanor saw those stacked on the bright green lawn she carried them back into the house.

It took her a long time. When it was done her arms felt yards longer and her whole bedroom was filled to the ceiling.

When her ma saw that, she thought to herself, *Enough! Had one fool bookworm to live with for thirty years, don't need another.* And that was that. She made it clear to Eleanor that her boy Jim was moving in and her daughter had to find somewhere else to live.

When Eleanor emerged from the bathroom, her strawberry blonde locks, normally so free, were teased and tortured into a pile on top of her head. She wore a short skirt that did nothing for her very thin legs. The skirt was pink and so was the matching waistcoat with gold buttons down the front.

No two ways about it – she was part hooker, part faded country and western star. And what she really wanted to be, just for today, was Congolese.

Flambeau could not, for the life of him, disguise his dismay.

# The Dance

Flambeau prayed for the ground at Broadwater Farm to open up and swallow him. He and Eleanor crept towards the gate and through it, watched by a million pairs of disparaging eyes.

They sat at a small white plastic table. He drank a coke, she a ginger ale. They avoided one another's gaze. They were curled in on themselves while fierce, unwelcoming shapes fluttered at their edges.

Then the music began. No one danced at first. Eleanor took a deep breath. 'Let's dance,' she said.

Flambeau looked at her as if she were mad. There was not a soul on the dance floor. She might be mad but she was also committed, fatally so.

'Right here. Right now,' she said. She got up and the poor boy had no choice but to follow.

Every eye in the place was on them as they made their way across the grass. It felt to him like a kind of execution by witness.

They danced dispiritedly at first, but the music was loud; it sent vibrations through the floor and into their feet. Pretty soon she reached for his hand and they moved easy and smooth together like they had, momentarily, in their practice.

A couple of the younger people smiled. She couldn't be so bad if she could Rhumba like that. One girl got up and joined them on the dance floor. Others soon followed.

Before they knew it the dance floor was stuffed with bodies and when she looked across at him, Flambeau was as alight as he ever had been in his small life. He even hugged her.

Flambeau was taking a break and sucking up a glass of lemonade when he saw Knight at the edge of the dance floor.

He was watching Eleanor with a proprietary eye. Flambeau could tell he liked what he saw.

Eleanor saw him too. She hesitated for a moment, but she didn't stop dancing. She drew Knight in with the flick of her hips, *one . . . three, four, one . . . three four.*

Knight slipped onto the dance floor. Flambeau followed.

Eleanor moved more intensely as Knight made his way towards her. She was breathtakingly sexy and spot on the beat as she ground her hips and lifted her arms in abandon. She surprised him. Even her pink outfit was somewhat tamed by the colour around her.

It was all going to be okay.

Knight moved closer. His face was alive with the excitement of claiming her. She was his and she was there.

The last time he looked at her like that was in her doorway that first time he had reached forward to touch her nipples with his long fingers.

Today was even better because today she had walked across the bridge between their two worlds. It was one of the sweetest victories of her life.

And it was over much too quickly.

★

When the woman came, she danced too close to Knight for Eleanor to ignore her. She slipped up and down his body as if she owned it.

Eleanor stopped dancing.

Flambeau saw her take a deep breath. He understood, as she did, that the lascivious dance was a declaration of war.

Eleanor was ready for it. In fact she made the first move.

'*Haai. Haai. Haai!*' shrieked the woman when Eleanor pushed her hard from behind.

The woman whipped around to face her assailant and said, '*Does anyone know this piece of rubbish?*' She looked Eleanor up and down as if she had floated up in the drain.

Flambeau pushed through adult legs to see. He could tell Eleanor had no idea what the woman had asked.

She looked around for Knight and called out to him, 'What did she say?'

He did not answer.

The woman looked straight at Knight and this time she addressed her question to him and in English, she asked, 'You know this bitch?'

Knight said nothing. A murmur ran through the crowd.

Flambeau looked at his hero and he waited for him to do the right thing. He waited for him to take Eleanor's hand and honour her.

She was plucked-chicken vulnerable.

But Knight did not move or speak or claim his love. Time stopped moving inside their world even as it clattered by just outside it. Knight still did not move.

Flambeau pushed through the people and took his place beside Eleanor. He spoke very quietly. 'I do. I know her.'

Eleanor couldn't breathe, let alone make sense of what the child had done. All she could see was Knight's face as he denied her.

Her love. The man for whom she held the deepest and most obliterating passion turned away from her.

Knight spoke to Flambeau in English so she could understand. Each word was separate and distinct. He said, 'If you know her – then – take – her – away.'

Then he turned around and walked away himself.

Eleanor and Flambeau watched Knight go.

Then Eleanor looked down and saw Flambeau's hand in hers.

The Congolese woman started dancing again, a slow lascivious shuffle. It was her victory dance.

Eleanor had to go. She very gently disengaged her hand from Flambeau's and stumbled across the grass in her gold high heels.

# The Black Hat

Flambeau sat on the grass and wept for Eleanor. He rocked as the sun sank lower in the sky. If he had been home he would have heard the parrots shriek and seen their bright green shapes flashing amongst the trees as they settled for the night. He cried for the loss of that comfort.

A shadow fell over his face. Flambeau opened his eyes like slits to see the shape of a hat moving there against the sun. There was something familiar about it. He sat up.

The man turned this way and that in his conversation. Then Flambeau got a flash of the man's face. It was Manu the Trafficker.

Flambeau shot to his feet and the words were out of his mouth before he could even think. '*Where's my mother?*'

The man looked at him in surprise.

Flambeau's voice was shaking when he asked again, '*Where is she?*'

The man glanced around and said, '*I don't know what you are saying, child.*'

'*She paid you to bring her to me,*' said Flambeau. '*But you did not do that.*'

The child turned to scour the milling crowd. He was looking for

Knight. But Knight was gone and Flambeau was on his own. The child shouted out in desperation, '*He's got my mama. This man has go—*'

'*Hey!*' A sharp voice sounded behind him. Flambeau turned to see a tall man loom over him.

'*What's all this fucking noise?*' the man hissed, and moved into the sunlight.

Flambeau's ten-year-old mind remembered this face. The way it had looked when it left Knight bleeding on the floor of his office. When it had walked down the passage towards the cowering Postman.

Deo's face.

Flambeau knew he was deadly.

When Deo knelt down to his eye level and said softly, '*I'm Deo, from Kinshasa,*' and held out his hand in a respectful African greeting, Flambeau's internal warning siren shrieked.

Flambeau looked at the man's hand and then at his face and without taking his hand he said, '*I know who you are.*'

Deo waited for the handshake. He insisted on it with his silence. Flambeau took the hand in spite of himself.

Deo's skin felt paper dry, like the shed skin of a snake. Whispery dry.

Flambeau asked, '*Where is my mother?*'

Deo said quietly, '*It is better not to know.*'

Flambeau drew his hand back as if it had been bitten.

Deo held his up in mock surrender. '*Okay. Okay. So you want to see your mama?*'

Flambeau nodded his head warily.

'*Been a long time?*' asked Deo.

'*It has been long,*' said Flambeau. His heart felt slick with new blood, full to overflowing. It ached.

'*Then we'll just have to make that happen, won't we, homeboy?*' Deo stood up to go. '*Come on.*'

Flambeau hesitated a moment. He looked around again for Knight.

Flambeau could not have known that Knight was watching him at that very moment.

That he saw every step of Deo's odious seduction of the boy. That he had to bite his hand to stop himself from stepping out into the fray. He knew that if he was to have the slightest chance against Deo, he would have to wait.

Eleanor put one foot in front of the other in the hope of finding some respite from her burning shame.

She caught sight of herself in the reflection of a shop window and she didn't know who it was except that, when she lifted her hand, so did the strange woman in the pink miniskirt.

She stooped to take off the gold shoes. She left them on the pavement and walked on barefoot.

The man from the nearby estate agency ran after her to give them back, but she waved him away and continued.

In spite of the ghosts waiting on the roof of her house in Kinlochbervie, that was where she wanted to be. She longed so fiercely for the biting cold of the beach that when she stumbled over the meagre canal that ran across the north of the city, she was grateful for its water.

She waded in until it was up to her knees. She held her hands under the surface so her face was close enough to the water for her to smell the algae and the mud.

An old lady passing by thought she must surely have lost her mind.

She was still dripping wet when she walked up to the door of the minicab office.

She did not greet anyone. She walked straight through to the office at the back and opened the door.

Postman looked up at her from his place behind the desk.

She rocked on her bare feet in the doorway. He got up slowly.

He knew her state without her saying a word. He walked over to the kettle and turned it on for tea.

# The Knight

When you grow up in Bukavu you don't expect to find shops and businesses built into railway arches. Well, in London they are. For miles, all across the city, you find car-repair joints and plumbers tucked under dark-brick railway arches.

The one Deo took Flambeau to had a faded advert for the *Dyeing of Clothes and Upholstery* hung over the door.

Inside, huge washing machines swished and groaned as they dyed the clothing scarlet, blue and pink. One machine kicked into spin cycle and burped its liquid into an open channel that disappeared under the floor. It was medieval.

Where on God's earth had they brought him?

Flambeau turned to Deo and asked, '*Where's my mother?*'

Deo simply looked at him and, with none of his former charm, indicated that Manu should take him away.

Flambeau called out, '*Where is she?*'

Neither man answered his question. Manu lifted a bunch of keys off a hook on the wall. Flambeau made a dash for the door.

But he had only gone three steps when he saw Deo looming in his path. The Trafficker brought his enormous fist down on the back of Flambeau's head with a crack.

It was so dark when Flambeau woke that he could see nothing at all. He could hear the rush of water and the rumble of machines. Beyond all that, he heard voices. The dark made his hearing more acute. He heard Knight's voice.

He began to scream. The sound that came out of his mouth was a bit like the jackals in the bush outside Bukavu. Sharp and high – half laugh, half cry.

He would have screamed until his voice was completely used up so that Knight would know he was there. But it wasn't long before a light went on and a hand plucked him from his prison.

The dye shop felt ferociously bright after all that darkness. So bright that Flambeau took some time to distinguish Knight's tall form from the others. He took immediate refuge behind it.

He felt Knight's hand reach back for him and hold him close.

Flambeau rested his head in the small of Knight's back. It was like leaning against a shade tree in the heat. In that moment Flambeau forgave Knight his betrayal of Eleanor. He had come after all. He was here.

'*Don't get too comfortable, boy,*' hissed Manu.

Knight tucked Flambeau closer still behind him and turned to look at Deo. The two men were silent for a moment. Then Knight asked quietly, '*Was his mother one of yours?*'

The older man looked at Knight, cocksure and vicious. '*How old were you when I found you looking through the fence of that Nganda in Kinshasa?*'

Knight did not heed the question, but eyed Deo warily.

Deo turned to Flambeau and said, '*He was sure he was going to be the greatest Sapeur of all time, this one. But he had nothing in his pocket. Not even one cent.'*

'*And you stole him,*' Flambeau said.

Deo smiled. '*I was his travel agent.*' His laugh echoed loud in the room. '*Him and your mother.*'

Knight took a deep breath and said very calmly, '*Tell us where she is and then we will leave.*'

Deo spun round like a snake and hissed, '*And who are you to ask me for anything?*'

'*Fucking nobody,*' added Manu.

Knight looked down at his hands. '*You can have a Mercedes SRV in three months, Deo. Or new season Louis Vuitton.*' Knight continued, 'Postman and I have a good thing going.'

Deo glanced around sharply. He snapped, '*If it is yours it is mine already.*'

Knight looked at Deo with a steady gaze. '*Not this time.*'

There was something authoritative in his voice that even Deo heard.

Knight smiled. '*The money is in the bank, Deo.*' Knight's voice did not betray his lie. He watched the uncertainty flicker across Deo's face. Then the Trafficker said, '*The Mercedes. AND you will bring me one more like Fatima.*'

Flambeau turned to stone.

Knight glanced at the frozen boy. He could feel him understanding.

Deo said, '*After all, if you take one away, you must give me one back.*'

The silence in the room hummed with danger. Flambeau did not dare to look at his hero. His swiftly falling hero.

'*Yes. One more,*' said Knight quietly.

The child whispered, '*You sold Fatima.*' He looked at Knight then and silent tears ran down his cheeks.

Knight did not meet his gaze or answer his question.

A fury grew inside Flambeau's grief. A shame. Both he and Eleanor had lost their hearts to Knight. He had required them to love him. He had loved them both back so fully that they couldn't imagine a world without him. Only then had he revealed what he was made of.

Rage tore through Flambeau. It made him bold and also foolhardy. When Knight reached for the boy's hand, Flambeau lashed out at him. He got to his feet and hissed, '*Get away from me.*'

All he could hear beyond the raucous thumping of his heart was Deo's poisonous laughter.

A knock sounded at the dye shop door.

No one moved to answer it. Another knock. Deo nodded to Manu and he opened the door.

A gas and electricity man stood there in his blue overall. 'I have to read your meter, mate.'

It was so out of another world, this hopeful face, that he swept past them before they could object.

The meter reader put his toolbag down under the ancient electricity meter suspended on the wall and began to scratch for the key to open it. It was only then that the chill in the room hit him.

He turned slowly to take in the tableau of frozen men around him and the weeping, visibly shaking boy.

Then Deo said, 'Why don't you come back tomorrow?'

'Yeah. Okay.' The meter reader shoved his tools into the bag and headed for the door.

Knight's question hardly slowed him. 'What's your next stop, mate?'

'Hackney,' said the meter reader. 'Oswald Road.'

'My son's going to football practice in Stoke Newington. It's on your way,' said Knight.

Flambeau looked at Knight in utter bewilderment. The meter reader was in a panic.

'Can he ride with you?' asked Knight.

Deo and Manu exchanged looks.

The meter reader whispered, 'Okay.'

Knight turned to Deo and said, 'The address. Now.' He tore an old receipt out of his wallet and held it out. *'What do you say, Deo?'*

Deo was uncertain for a moment and then he snapped, *'I say no. Because you lie about the money and the girl. You're a liar!'*

Knight's knife was out and against Manu's stomach before he could blink.

The knife tip made a small incision and blood coloured Manu's shirt.

A freezing blast of terror hit Flambeau in his gut when he saw it. Now what?

Knight twisted Manu's arm until he sank to his knees. Then, in a move as sudden as it was skilled, he thrust his knife into the back of Manu's hand.

No one moved.

Knight shouted, 'A pen.'

No one responded. Knight turned to the meter reader and hissed, 'Give me your pen!'

The meter reader unclipped the pen from his top pocket and handed it to Knight.

Manu searched Deo's face for permission. The blood seeped out of the wound in his hand. It seemed to Flambeau like hours were passing.

Deo finally nodded. Manu scribbled the address on the paper. He didn't even stand up to hand it over, but just left it there on the floor and rolled away from it.

Knight said, '*Get it, Flambeau.*'

But the boy was frozen in terror. He also saw the threat gathering behind Knight.

Knight said, '*Get it. Now!*'

The boy crouched down to pick up the piece of paper, speckled with Manu's blood. He did not take his eyes off Deo and the lieutenant huddled at the door all beast-like bent and curved.

Was that a tail he saw thrashing on the floor behind them?

Yes, a thick black tail of animal hair.

Flambeau cried out to Knight. He could tell that he saw it too.

Knight crouched down in front of the frozen boy and whispered, '*Go.*'

Flambeau shook his head. He could not have said it in words, but the child could see what Knight was doing for him. It made the love he had for him well up and wash clean all the bad things he had done. He would not leave him.

Knight kissed Flambeau's head and mumbled thick with feeling, '*Go now. I'll come later.*'

Flambeau looked up at him.

Knight fought to control the fear in his eyes. '*Don't tell her where I am. Okay?*'

The boy nodded.

Knight growled, '*It's not a good place for her.*'

Flambeau touched Knight's face in an oddly grown-up gesture.

Knight stood up.

Flambeau held on to him.

It took a huge effort to prise his hands loose.

Flambeau stumbled to the door and followed the trembling meter reader outside.

Knight turned to face the two men. Terror churned his insides, but he wasn't going to let them see his fear. He took a long deep breath, looked straight into Deo's eyes and spoke quietly. '*I know more about you than anyone walking the earth. I will tell it all. Every child you sold. Every woman. Every boy.*'

It pleased Knight to see a flash of fear in Deo's eyes. '*I will see you sit in jail until you are a lonely old man with grey fluff in your ears and worms in your stomach.*'

Deo was grave for a moment and then he laughed.

He laughed loudly.

The sound of his laughter reached Flambeau who was climbing into the truck. Then he heard his name ring out, '*Hey, Flambeau.*'

The child stopped.

'*That paper will get you nowhere,*' shouted Deo.

Flambeau turned to scan the windows of the dye shop, but he could see no one.

Deo called out again, '*But I know where she is. Come! It will take us only a few hours on a bus and you will be together again.*'

Flambeau climbed down off the truck. His longing overcame his distrust and he began to walk back towards the building.

Deo watched his approach through the window.

Knight's face was rigid.

Deo turned to him and said, '*I will have the boy when you are gone.*'

He motioned to his lieutenant to open the door for the child. Then Deo turned to Knight and said, '*He will take your place.*'

A sharp, long-buried memory filled the silent slipstream left by

Deo's words. The night before he had brought them to London all those years ago, Deo sealed his absolute power over the boys. He took first Postman and then Knight into the corrugated hut that passed as their temporary home and he stole their last remaining dignity.

Knight sucked in the bitter air around that terrible fact. And then in a sudden, unstoppable rush of fury, he roared, '*Run, Flambeau. Run!*'

The boy heard Knight's cry, and turned to flee.

Knight broke onto Deo's body like a wave. He locked his arms around his neck and drove his knife so deep into his chest that his hand disappeared.

Flambeau looked back when he reached the door of the truck. Through the open door he saw Deo slip out of Knight's arms and onto the floor.

Then Flambeau saw the horns.

They had horns. The two raging men who encircled his cowering friend had horns on the side of their heads where their ears should have been.

# Nothing

Flambeau's small body moved lightly, so lightly he seemed to float, ephemeral, in the murk of the darkened living room.

Eleanor lifted her head and saw his face move through the darkness towards her. It was a terrible face.

She still wore her pink outfit, but it didn't feel like it belonged to her any more. She had shrunk inside it. She got up clumsily, moved towards him and whispered, 'Where is he?'

Flambeau hesitated. Then he shook his head. She took the slip of paper out of his hand. What she saw there made no sense. 'What the hell is this?'

Flambeau looked up at her, but he didn't speak. He was not even sure that he could.

She looked at the paper again. She didn't know what it meant. 'This is an address in Scotland.'

He looked at her and said, 'What?'

'Oh Flambeau, it's nowhere. It's a truck-stop on the edge of the sea. Dad and I drove past it every time we went to Inverness.'

The remaining life drained from his eyes and he whispered, 'Then it was for nothing.' He looked at her in horror.

It came to her then that this feeling of heat in the centre of her thudding chest that spread to the palms of her hands and the soles of her feet was what Flambeau had felt for half a year after he was taken from his mother.

She asked, 'Where is he, lad? It doesn't matter about the woman. I just want to find him. Please.'

He could see that she was unravelling when she said it again. 'Please.'

The thing is, if you've seen death often enough you can smell it coming ever after. He knew the end when he saw it. He spoke softly, matter of factly, simply. 'They had horns and tails.'

Ah God! She lashed out. A lamp fell over. She grabbed for it, tripped, hit her head. And then she cried.

Flambeau helped her to sit up. She opened her arms to him. He curled up there and, at last, he wept into her bony chest.

The sky was dark indigo with rain and grief that breaking dawn.

The silhouette of a body swung dark against the slim red streaks of sky. It was Knight's beautiful body and it was impaled on a stake in the middle of the soccer fields of Broadwater Farm.

# Part Three

# Sleep

The whole damned housing estate looked lifeless after that. Bleak grey buildings against a bleaker sky.

If Eleanor and Flambeau had been able to see straight they would have noticed the messengers bringing news of his death. They would have watched them scatter this way and that, as if blown by the wind: dark shapes, made darker by their tidings.

Eleanor heard distant knocking, but she couldn't have told you if they were knocking on her door.

Laetitia came every day. She knocked and waited and knocked again. But Flambeau and Eleanor could not have received her even if they had wanted to.

They climbed under the duvet and didn't move for three days. The beads on the big pink lamp beside her bed tinkled and it sounded like bones.

Postman came too. He knocked. He looked in the window. Then he moved away.

Later, Eleanor wished she had known it was him, because she would have opened the door and had him join their bleak house.

Instead, Postman went onto the roof. He went into the corner to seek protection from the bitter wind. His longing for Knight sat there with him. He rocked and groaned with it.

Eleanor slept. She slept like an animal in winter because she would not have survived if she had been awake. And she slept in the hope that when she woke up, Knight would be there.

Flambeau lay next to her, but he was sleepless most of the time. He blinked and longed for the peace of unconsciousness, but it eluded him.

The child's thoughts and feelings roamed so vast and terrible a distance while Eleanor slept, that most adults would have been led to the brink by such a journey. After three days he lifted the covers off his fully clothed body and slipped out of the room.

He sat at the kitchen table, but he didn't find it any better there. A knock sounded at the door, but he had long lost the ability to respond. Then Laetitia appeared at the kitchen window. She knocked on the glass. He turned to see her there.

Flambeau opened the window. She handed him a heavy pot. He nearly dropped it as he took its full weight. He nodded his thanks. Then he turned away from her. She could see that words were beyond him.

Flambeau sat on the bed gingerly. He rested his back against the wall where the bedstead should have been. He picked the tray off the floor beside the bed. It contained two plates of thick pondu. He rested it on his lap.

He called her name, 'Eleanor.'

It was a soft and kind sound, but she wished with every remaining live cell in her body that he had been saying '*Chérie*'.

She sat up.

He handed her a plate, but she couldn't take it.

Her stomach felt like a sliver.

He put it back on the tray.

He put his plate back on the tray too.

He put the tray on the floor and then they sat there like ghosts. Barely breathing.

On the fourth morning, Flambeau walked into the hallway to see a funeral notice on the floor under the post flap. It had a smiling photo of Knight at the top of the page.

Then he heard the birds. He swore later that they had heard news of Knight's death and were wailing.

He waited for the walkway outside the flat to be deserted before he opened the door. He blinked. Paused. Then he walked up the stairs with his hand on the wall for support and through the red door.

The food trays in the birdcage were empty. Flambeau filled them to the brim with seed. He filled the water bowl too. He filled Sally's trough with the remaining cat food and then he realised she was gone.

He sat on the box in the corner.

The birds sat on his shoulders.

He cried. He cried. He cried until his body shook with sobs even when the crying had stopped.

It was only when he crossed to the far side of the roof that Flambeau found Postman in his corner bent over and crippled with the shock of his aloneness.

He sat beside him for a while.

Neither spoke.

Postman put out his hand and Flambeau took it.

Flambeau worked for two days to prepare for the funeral. He hand-washed his only good shirt and trousers and he put them out to dry. Then he ironed them very carefully.

Eleanor opened her eyes briefly to see him ironing her dress. It sent her right back into her defensive slumber.

On the morning of the funeral Flambeau got dressed. He put Knight's gold chain around his neck. Then he came to get Eleanor.

She couldn't move. He stood beside her bed and he said, 'It's time.'

She looked at him and she wanted to speak, but her teeth felt as if they had turned to dust in her mouth and there was no chance her skull wouldn't follow if she tried to move it.

He gently pulled the duvet back. He took her hand and he pulled her up to a sitting position.

Later she would be grateful to him for rousing her, but she wasn't at the time.

She was lost.

It would be a long time before she forgave herself for leaving that poor child to grieve alone.

She knew what he must have had to overcome that morning to sit her skeletal body in the bath and sponge her down.

The amazing thing was that he somehow knew that she had to be at that funeral if she was going to stand a chance. He wasn't going to let her go there stinking of grief.

He chose her outfit. He told her she had to put some lipstick on or they would bury her instead.

He was Congolese after all, and the Congolese look like a million dollars even if they are laying one of their own to rest.

Maybe especially then, when they are at their most vulnerable. Maybe it marks them as the ones that are still breathing.

# Goodbye

Flambeau and Eleanor huddled together on the pew in the back of the church, shrunk to almost nothing. Their eyes were down. They were silent.

It felt to both of them as if they hadn't spoken for a year. Shadows ebbed and flowed on their faces as mourners passed them in their finery.

Postman, transformed once more into smooth Sapeur by his black silk jacket, stopped at the end of their pew. They looked up to see him.

He opened his arms and waited there like a vast bird, insistent.

Flambeau was first to rise.

Eleanor followed, and as she entered Postman's expansive embrace she smelt his warmth and his succour.

The baptismal font was afire with floating candles. There were more on the floor.

The singing was pure African leave-taking, deep and ceremonial.

Postman led them down the aisle to the very front of the church.

The whole congregation rumbled their approval with stamping feet as they stepped forward to take their place in the family pew.

There was someone else sitting there alongside them and she was as hollowed out as they were. It was Knight's other woman, barefaced in her grief.

Eleanor looked at her and she seemed so small and so shrunken she wondered how she could ever have feared her. She saw in her gaze that she was thinking the same of her.

The widows.

Eleanor nodded to her. She wished that she knew her name. The woman held her gaze. She would have nodded back if she could have.

When Flambeau watched Pastor Gold Tooth splash water off the end of a slim branch onto the mourners as he walked down the aisle he remembered 'snake boy'.

He watched warily as the Pastor splashed Laetitia, Elvira, Arsenne and the two younger girls. Didier was not with them.

When Flambeau looked at his cousins he wondered who they were, really. It wasn't because they were so changed. It was he who had become someone else.

The church was packed. So many people had loved Knight or at least had been in love with his charm and his charisma. They had all come to take their leave.

Gold Tooth splashed the Charismatic Born Agains and the Catholics. He blessed the Sapeurs, dressed to the nines, those who didn't know one end of a church from another and those who did. And then he turned to the 'family' whom Knight had loved.

He splashed the other woman first. He hesitated for a second before he splashed Eleanor. She could see that he was unsure if he should. She looked at him and nodded. Please.

The water felt soft on her skin. She thought it would be cold, but it felt warm and it smelt of honeysuckle. They put a drop of sweet-smelling oil in there just to make it so.

Gold Tooth splashed Postman who lowered his head the better to feel the water. He wept.

Eleanor put a hand on his sobbing back.

The Pastor splashed Flambeau's head and hands and then, most extraordinarily, he half knelt at the child's feet.

It was an act of public apology, and the church went utterly silent. The water dripped. The candles flickered. Flambeau looked at the top of the man's head for a long time.

When he glanced at his Aunt Laetitia he could see she was giving him permission to make his own decision. That it would be okay with her if he withheld the grace of his forgiveness. Then he looked at Eleanor.

Her face reminded him that their recent suffering made this small despot and his cruelty irrelevant.

Flambeau touched the top of the Pastor's head in forgiveness, and the man shuffled awkwardly to his feet.

Laetitia's voice rang out and before long the music was back to its prior fullness.

The Pastor led the family to the coffin.

The Woman went first. She knelt with perfect dignity and touched Knight's cheek. Then she crossed her heart and stepped away.

Postman followed, and as he bade his brother farewell he took his hand and kissed it.

Flambeau and Eleanor stepped up to the coffin together. Neither could have achieved it alone. Neither was ready for what they saw there.

★

Knight's face looked as if he had come to the end of a journey and was at peace with it.

His beauty was still breathtaking, the round stretch of skin over his cheekbones and the dip of his cheeks underneath them just as they were. But it was also true that he didn't look like himself. He looked like a hotel room that once contained raucous life and was now scattered with used towels and a forgotten hairbrush. He was no longer there.

To say that it enraged Eleanor would be a monumental understatement. It was the first and only time she felt as if she were melting with fury, that her eyes were filling with liquid ore. It made her want to hit him.

She held onto the sides of the coffin to stop herself doing something as crazy as that, but she must have made a terrible sound because Flambeau reached for her hand.

When she finally got a grip on herself she saw Gold Tooth had shielded her body from the congregation for just long enough to hide the grimace that tore her face in two and made her hideous with suffering.

And still Knight did not open his eyes and laugh and call her *chérie*.

It was then, in that small moment, she understood, finally, that he was dead.

Flambeau was the bearer of many tender mercies. That moment he did not look away from her grief in embarrassment or disgust, and so showed her the greatest mercy of all.

He invited her into the world that he and Knight had occupied, the community of those who knew how bad things can be. He made her one of them and by so doing gave her a tomorrow.

She came to be grateful to Flambeau for that. But she wasn't grateful that day, nor for a long time afterwards. That day she did not want a tomorrow.

Flambeau remained at the side of the coffin while Eleanor returned to her seat.

He leaned down and kissed Knight's forehead. Then he whispered in Lingala, '*Melesi, Papa. Thank you.*'

The Pastor lifted his branch.

The drops of water landed in the boy's soft black hair; they landed complete and individual on Knight's loved, loved face and thereby wove the two of them together.

The boy felt the arrival of a new ancestral presence in his inner world. And he shuddered.

# Pink Suitcase

The rain was pelting down when they stepped out of the church. It was a hard rain for London. And it was cold.

People scattered like leaves. The entire congregation seemed to have been swept away in the time it took to open an umbrella.

Only Flambeau, Eleanor and Postman were left.

They stood in the middle of the small square. No one had the slightest idea what to do next.

Flambeau took Eleanor's hand.

She said, 'Can't go home.'

The truth was neither of them could have crossed the threshold of their flat, so full of unmade beds and mourning and sweat and dissolution. The distance they had travelled from morning to afternoon made it fatal to go backwards.

It seemed to occur to both of them at the same time that Postman needed a home. He would sweep out the ghosts with his sweetness and make it safe.

Eleanor squashed her keys into Postman's hand.

Postman asked, 'What is this?'

She said, 'You can't sleep on the floor in that office any more. You'll grow mould.'

Postman laughed. 'I like the floor.'

'Then sleep on mine,' she said.

'Where will you sleep?' asked Postman.

Eleanor looked at him. 'I don't know yet.'

Postman nodded. He pulled a cheque out of his pocket and gave it to Eleanor. She glanced at the name written there and shook her head.

'No.'

Postman shrugged. 'You might need it, sister.'

Flambeau looked up at her: he wanted to tell her that Sylvia Harrison wouldn't mind if she used it to advance their journey, that she would understand about his mother. But her face was so full of feeling he held his tongue.

Postman turned to ruffle Flambeau's hair. Flambeau wrapped his arms around Postman's waist.

Eleanor stepped forward to join their embrace. Flambeau was sandwiched between their two adult bodies. Eleanor laid her head on Postman's shoulder then lifted her head to look at him. His eyes were sad and still. She ran her hand across his cheek.

Postman gave Flambeau one last squeeze and then turned to walk away. He looked back briefly and said 'Ta . . .', then he walked again. They watched him until he disappeared.

Uncertainty flooded through Eleanor when he had gone. She sat on the church steps and put her head in her hands, Sylvia Harrison's cheque forgotten in her lap.

'Come with me. Please,' said Flambeau.

'Ah no, Flambeau,' she murmured.

Flambeau scratched in his pocket and pulled out the piece of paper Manu had written the address on. He held it out to her. 'What else is there for us?'

Eleanor could see Flambeau's face was full of purpose and she knew that she had none.

She needed someone with a mission because her own single imperative was to stop the burning in the palms of her hands. She would happily have drowned herself in the canal to get rid of that unbearable feeling.

So if the address he handed to her had been in France or in Birmingham she would have leapt at the chance to go somewhere else.

But it wasn't: it was down the road from her pa's house in Kinlochbervie. Now what were the chances of that?

All that awaited her there was another dead face to remember. It wasn't even as if she thought about it. Her father just loomed, and she shrank, and that was that. She knew she would not make it out of there with her full wits about her.

She looked up at the child and all she could think to say was, 'I don't have a toothbrush.'

'Don't move,' he said, and he was gone.

She wished she had said more to stop him, but it seemed as if she would need to be Hercules to explain about the dead face waiting for her up there in the North.

When Flambeau came across the square towards Eleanor pulling her pink suitcase his eyes were shining because he was on his mission once more. He came closer and, with great pride, he gave her the forged driver's licence with Sylvia's name on it.

Eleanor blurted out, 'I can't come with you, Flambeau.'

He stopped in his tracks to consider her words, then brushed them aside. 'I packed socks and pyjamas. And a toothbrush.'

He looked at her, eyes pleading.

She looked only at her feet.

He saw the bones in her face: the plane of her forehead, the round fists of her cheekbones, shockingly prominent. She was not far from skull.

She whispered, 'Can't go back there. Sorry.'

He hung his head for a moment then he handed her the suitcase, turned, and began to walk away.

She watched him.

Was that it?

Was that all the fight he had in him?

After all that they had done for one another. Outrage bubbled through her body. It brought her back from the nearly dead. Maybe he knew it would.

When she came belting around the corner with her suitcase bouncing unwieldy behind her she was sick with fear that she had lost Flambeau. He was not anywhere to be seen.

She stopped. The pounding in her heart started up like machine-gun fire. She shouted, 'Flambeau!'

And a small voice behind her answered, 'Here.'

She turned to see him sitting on the steps behind her. She felt the pink sweep across her face, 'What the hell are you doing?'

He looked up at her. Then down at his feet. 'Waiting for you.'

She sat on the step beside him. Hung her head for a moment, and then she laughed.

It didn't even really feel like laughter but it was, at least, its pale cousin.

He smiled at her.

She stood up and headed towards the High Street. Flambeau called out, 'Where are you going?'

She shouted, 'Where do you think?'

Flambeau followed Eleanor's pink suitcase along the pavement, across the railway bridge and into the door of the post office. He had visited this very post office with Laetitia. He knew it was manned by a married couple who enlivened their tedious days with verbal combat. Their vicious banter frightened Flambeau and he wished Eleanor hadn't chosen this branch, but he knew that interrupting the force of her motion held even greater peril.

It was a small post office tucked between an off-licence and a newsagent. The two combatants moved with brilliant delicacy in the small space behind the counter. Never brushing hands, never colliding, never asking for one another's help. Two entirely separate planets.

'You order the first-class stamps, Tony?' said the wife.

'No.'

'Why not?'

'You said you'd do it.'

As Eleanor approached the counter the woman held out her hand for the cheque and driver's licence without even glancing up at her face; not for a moment was she diverted from the battle with her spouse. 'No, I didn't, Tony.'

'Yes, you did, Ellen.'

'No, I didn't.'

'You always do the orders.'

'No, I bloody don't.'

'You do, you know.'

'What notes d'you want, love?' the woman asked Eleanor without skipping a beat.

It took Eleanor a moment to realise the woman was talking to her. She thought about it and then she mumbled, 'Don't care.'

The woman glanced up at the dullness in Eleanor's voice; it awakened her instinct for trouble. She glanced at the driver's licence and then at Eleanor's face.

At that moment a car pulled up outside the post office.

It wasn't the vehicle itself that intruded into their purpose, it was the music blasting from its very superior sound system. Music that snaked its way into the post office and wrapped itself around both Eleanor and Flambeau's aching hearts. It was Joseph Kabasele and his soulful rhumba.

With a thumping heart, Eleanor turned around to see where it was coming from. She saw the driver emerge from the car and float across the frosted window. He moved like a dancer. Even from his silhouette, she could tell he was a Sapeur.

Eleanor turned to look at Flambeau, and he could see in her eyes the hope that Knight had risen from the dead. He looked away.

Eleanor reached for Flambeau's hand.

The woman from the post office shook her head and muttered, 'Oh dear. Had one too many today then, have we?'

Flambeau seized on this explanation and nodded vigorously. The woman said, 'She should sleep it, lad. Take her home.'

Eleanor turned to see the car pull away and it made her want to run after it.

'Now how d'you want the money?' the wife asked Eleanor slowly, as if talking to a deaf person.

Again, it was Flambeau who mumbled, 'She'll take anything. Doesn't matter.'

The woman counted out the money and stuffed it under the glass.

'Thank you,' Eleanor finally whispered.

'Goodbye,' said Flambeau.

As they turned the pink suitcase around and began to walk past the now much longer queue, the wife said to the husband, 'You going to brew up some tea then, Tony?'

'No, Ellen.'

'Why not?'

'Made it yesterday, didn't I.'

'No, you didn't.'

'Yes, I did.'

It was only then that the wife noticed the forgotten driver's licence on the counter. She held it up and shouted at Eleanor's retreating back, 'Your licence, love!'

Eleanor paused only briefly. Without turning back she waved it away with her hand and then walked out onto the street.

# The Train

The need to sleep overtook Eleanor with the clamour of a fast-moving storm. She could have slept curled up on the top of a rubbish bin, she was so tired.

In contrast, Flambeau's capacity for wakefulness had expanded with the journey ahead. He had to keep things moving.

The noise of machines and people made her want to weep as they rubbed on her ears. She could not wait to get into that train and close her tortured eyes.

He was equally determined not to let her.

London was still streaming by the window when she felt soft oblivion just about to shut the door on the past four days of her life.

She felt the tug of his small hand on her shirt. 'Hey, Eleanor.'

'What?'

'It's Wembley Stadium. Look.'

'Night, Flambeau.'

A few minutes later when the bliss of sleep was looming once more he shouted, 'Eleanor.'

She jumped out of her skin. 'What?'

'You missed the bridge. It was a big bridge.'

She looked at him and her eyes narrowed. 'What's going on?'

'Nothing.'

'Oh bullshit, Flambeau. You can see I'm trying to sleep and you are not letting me. Why?'

He considered her for a moment. 'You can't go to sleep.'

'Why not?'

'Because you are very sad.'

'So?'

'So you might decide that you don't want to wake up.'

'And then?'

'And then I won't know where to get off the train.'

There it was, right there.

She was compelled to remain alive to finish the job of getting him where he needed to go.

She laughed.

If she wanted to sleep she was going to have to trick him.

Eleanor had learnt half of her vocabulary playing word games with her dad. There was no way Flambeau could match her ability in this domain. He was ten years old and English was his fourth language, for God's sake.

And so she began with, 'What does the word rudiments mean?'

Flambeau looked at her with a crinkle between his brows and he said, 'This is a game?'

She nodded. 'If I am the first to get to twenty you have to let me sleep.'

He looked at her and the killer in him lit up like a lamp. 'Say it again.'

'Rudiments.'

'Don't know. My turn.'

He thought for a moment and then he said, '*Mouchard.*'

'Not in French, Flambeau.'

He looked at her and he said. 'You speak yours, I speak mine.'

What could she say to that?

He spat out, '*Parapluie.*'

'Christ, how am I supposed to know that?'

Then she hit him with, 'Nuanced?'

'*Génisse.*'

'Esculent.'

'*Térébenthine.*'

'Hellbender.'

'*Amour?*' You would have thought she'd won the lottery the way she screamed. 'Love! I know that one. Love.'

He looked at her, smiled, and held up one finger. 'You have one.'

Big bloody deal! She could see that sleep was far, far away. Time for the big guns. 'Inamorata.'

'*Brebis.*'

'Ranid.'

'*Ecrire.*'

'Laconic.'

'*Genou.*'

'Homily.'

'*Cochon.*'

'Albumen.'

'Me, me, me. I know. That is the white part of the egg.'

She looked at him and he grinned. 'One and one. We are even.'

She was never going to sleep. And now that she stopped to think about it, she didn't feel tired any more.

It was he who stretched out on the bench and put his head as close to her lap as he could without it seeming as if he was seeking comfort. Then he closed his eyes and was asleep in seconds.

She watched him breathe in and out as the day turned to dusk and then to night.

# *Scotland*

By the time morning came Eleanor was so sleep-deprived that she walked into a pillar at Inverness station.

It was raining. Pelting down. And they were both starving.

When she had travelled on shopping trips to Inverness as a child with her dad, they would stop for tea in the hotel just alongside the station.

She took Flambeau there for a bowl of porridge. He was as eager as a whippet. She was leaden with the burden of what lay ahead.

Now that she was actually here, or near enough, she was certain their search would lead to nothing.

Flambeau's animation told her he believed absolutely that they were closing in. 'I'm going to take Mama to Dolce and Gabbana,' he said.

Oh, those words came out of his mouth with exactly the same intonation and sense of wonder with which Knight had spoken them. They were so full of promise her stomach churned.

He said, 'I know where it is. I looked on the map.' His eyes shone. 'Sloane Street. I'm going to take her to Sloane Street and buy her a pair of shoes to make her proud.'

Eleanor looked into her bowl of porridge. 'Sometimes we can't do what we most want to do, Flambeau.'

There, she had said it.

He looked at her as if she were speaking Greek.

It was a look that insisted on clarification.

She said, 'We may not find her, lad.'

He shook his head. 'Fatima, I will never find. I will never find her because she was sold to the Arabs and I don't know the way to their country.'

'How do you know that?' she asked.

He looked at his hands and swallowed, 'Deo.'

It came to Eleanor then that the only reason Deo didn't sell Flambeau to the Arabs when Manu first got him to London was that he was after a bigger prize. He wanted Bijou. And he would only get her if her son arrived in London safely.

And he did get her. Knight was right: Flambeau would never see his mother again.

It made Eleanor grab the child's hand and kiss it.

When she asked the waitress if the bus to Wick still left from the old depot the woman nodded and picked up a teaspoon from the dark-green carpet.

Eleanor waited for her to wipe it on her apron and put it back on the table. It came to her then that this was the table she and her father had chosen whenever they stopped by to eat here all those years ago. He was so alive then. So funny.

Eleanor showed the waitress the address on the piece of paper.

'That's not anywhere, lass. It's a truck stop. Don't know why anyone would want to go there. Just sea and sky,' she said.

'Aye. I thought as much.'

There was something of Eleanor's mother in the cautious way the waitress moved. But it was her hands, the exact, crinkled wornness of the skin that took Eleanor back to the house in Kinlochbervie.

Those hands had packed Eleanor's bags and sent her off to London. Those hands had tied her father to the bed to stop him walking to the off-licence in the middle of the night. Those hands.

Eleanor heard her father's voice calling her as he struggled to untie the ropes that tethered him to the bed. He called sweetly at first. Then came the names. 'Bitch. You are a bitch just like your mother. You are a nothing. Nothing.'

She decided then, in the way one decides to leave a husband or a job or a way of life, that she wasn't going to listen to that suffering any more. Nor that eviscerating abuse.

She walked into the bedroom and untied him. He looked at her face while she did it.

She was trying not to gag. Her father had messed his blue pyjamas.

Eleanor climbed onto the roof. She hoped the wind would blow the sight of him so fouled out of her mind. She climbed to the very highest part and looked out to sea.

Eleanor's pa had often followed her onto the roof, but not in quite the state he was in that night. Not in the grip of such acute withdrawal. He stood there in the eye of the storm and apologised to her.

'For what?'

'For everything.'

She just looked at him.

If she had already seen Flambeau touch the Pastor's head in forgiveness she might have managed that same act, but that all lay so far in her future that it was just a light on the horizon.

225

The wind and the rain hit them hard and howled. He reached for her hand to steady himself just as she turned away. She no longer knew the order of things. Had she turned away when his hand was out and needy or had she not seen it? Either way, she couldn't bear to see and smell the man he had become.

She was well gone by the time he fell. But she saw it in her mind's eye forever after. Completely silent. Slow and almost beautiful.

They ran all the way to the bus depot in the rain. Something about how they slopped through the puddles in their shoes without even trying to keep them dry made Eleanor laugh.

Then she couldn't stop laughing.

Flambeau took her hand to steady her and she called him Knight three times in a row. Then she burst into sudden tears. She hung her head between her knees so she didn't throw up.

Finally he looked at her and said, 'I think that you must sleep.'

She wasn't even sitting down before her eyes closed. She lay on the back row of the bus with her feet up against the glass and didn't move an inch for five hours.

This time he let her sleep. He watched his own reflection in the window glass and prayed.

He woke her when they hit the sea.

A dull factory ship floated in the grim metal swell. Machinery on board clanked and growled. Smaller fishing boats were attached to it like offspring.

Just as the doors of the bus were about to close Eleanor called out to the driver, 'When do you come back this way?'

The driver called out, 'Tuesday.'

Flambeau's small face was bursting with apprehension and excitement as he looked around him. But nothing made any sense.

A clutch of truck drivers were huddled around a caravan teashop.

Five long trucks were parked in the far corner. Beyond them were the sea and the factory ship.

Flambeau looked up at Eleanor. He needed her to explain, but she didn't like what she saw and she wasn't ready to say so. 'Let's go . . .' she said and took his hand.

A scantily clad African woman scuttled across the parking lot. Her short skirt and shiny-blue sequined top flashed absurd in the day that felt like night.

Flambeau let go of Eleanor's hand.

Oh God.

Eleanor didn't know what to say. She found herself putting her arms around the child's bony shoulders.

A few men, fishermen maybe, were gathered at the door of one of the large trucks.

One man came out, the other went in.

The African woman in the shiny blue skirt pushed past them and into the truck.

Flambeau said, 'She's from the Congo. I swear. See. The walk.'

Eleanor didn't want to see the walk. She took his arm. He would not let her shift him.

She didn't want to shout, but she did. 'We can't go in there, Flambeau.'

He looked up at her.

'Really, truly. We can't,' she whispered.

He saw the gravity in her face and stopped resisting.

'Come on. I'll buy you some hot chips,' she said.

He allowed her to guide him to the tea wagon.

# Jewel

They sat in the soft grey sand on the sheltered side of the tea wagon and ate.

Leftover chip papers and paper cups were scattered all around them. But beyond the rubbish were the moors and their thick dense band of green. It was wide open and clean.

A loud woman's voice called out behind them.

Flambeau sat up as if he had been stung. It came again. Then someone answered. It was indistinct Kinyarwanda thrown up into the wind, and it got him to his feet.

He stepped out of the shadow of the truck.

A woman walked slowly across the car park, head down, high heels, short skirt – tired items of allure.

She stopped in the middle of the parking lot. She lifted her head. What had she sensed? She began to turn. Her beautiful profile confirmed her identity.

It was she. It was his mother.

★

Flambeau was still. His mother was still too. Fine and still. No wonder the hyenas thought her such a prize.

The two of them were so similarly long and lean, so poised. Just then, it was as if she could somehow sense, but still not locate, her son.

Then a car hooter sounded and his mother looked away.

Flambeau saw her stumble in her high heels over to a silver car that was waiting there.

The car pulled off and she was gone before he had even opened his mouth.

He turned to face Eleanor and said, 'What kind of place is this?'

She couldn't answer that.

The door to the truck container beyond opened and a fisherman came out shouting in drunken Russian.

A naked African woman dancing a sad, provocative dance was visible before the door closed again.

Flambeau looked at Eleanor once more.

She looked at her feet.

He ran.

The two of them were absurdly small in the vast flatness of that windswept road beyond the truck stop. He was forced to wait for her to catch up.

'That's not my mother,' he said.

She stopped walking.

He turned to face her and spoke emphatically. 'My mother's name is Bijou. It means J-E-W-E-L.'

He half turned to her, then away, desperate. 'She teaches children to read and write. And she loves to dance.'

'No,' barked Eleanor.

He looked at her.

'She loves you. Above all else. She loves you.'

He searched her face and saw that she meant what she said, whether it was true or not.

He wanted it to be true.

The rain started up again. It was a fine, grey drizzle. The wind off the sea whipped it onto their faces.

She said, 'Do you want to be there when she gets back?'

He shrugged.

After a long silence Flambeau spoke. 'Why didn't she come and get me?'

Eleanor shook her head, 'Do you think she wanted it to be this way?'

He said nothing.

'Or me? D'you think I wanted to fall in love with Knight? And you. You and your bloody life.'

Flambeau turned to look at her.

She said it again, 'Do you?'

He spoke simply and his words sounded surprised. 'But you did.'

She looked at him against the ravaged black moor and she spoke the truth. 'Aye.'

He knew now that she loved him whether she wanted to or not. That it was the kind of love that meant that she always would.

Eleanor said, 'Sometimes grown-ups just can't do what they want most in the whole world.'

That is a terrible thing to know. She had thought he already knew it, what with all he had seen in his life. But he didn't. He believed his mother was always greater than the obstacles in her path. Until now.

He couldn't hold his face together any longer; it folded and crumpled. And he wept until it was pitch dark, night.

The next time Eleanor looked into Flambeau's eyes he was older by a decade. He needed to be for what lay ahead.

# The Blanket

Their wait was cold and full of bitter purpose. They sheltered in the shadow of the caravan where they could see the cars come and go.

When the silver car screeched to a halt they were ready.

Flambeau's mother got out. The car pulled off before she was even safely away from the door. She looked over at the sea for a moment. The full moon lit the water's gentle heaving.

Flambeau stepped out of the shadows and began to walk towards her. Before he could reach her or even call out she had disappeared into the mouth of one of the large trucks.

The door closed. Flambeau took a breath and walked towards it.

Eleanor watched his journey with her heart in her mouth. She waited for him to beckon to her to follow but he did not. She followed anyway.

He opened the door to the truck a crack and looked in. He saw a row of men on a bench, their backs to him. The sound of breathing beyond was rhythmical, obscene, even to his uneducated ears.

He slipped inside. Under the long bench he glimpsed the arm of a black woman on the metal floor of the truck. It jerked in time with the grunts, passively.

His eyes asked silently, what is happening here?

The row of bent backs masked his view.

He peered through the gaps between them and saw a mattress in the corner of the truck. His mother lay on it. The man on top of her thrust into her.

Oh God. Even though his view of the coupling was interrupted it made it no less crude, brutal, banal.

And it was witnessed by this row of men stooped low with waiting.

His mother turned her face away from the rank smell of the man's breath and he slapped it back.

She opened her gritted-shut eyes. And she saw Flambeau.

Disbelief and wonder passed over her face. She smiled, a flash, and then shame snatched it away.

She pushed the man off her. He rolled off into the shadows, drunk.

Flambeau tried to push through the waiting men. One man stopped him with his broad arm. Flambeau bit his hand. The man slapped the boy's face. His comrades rose in a clatter.

His mother shouted, fearful for him, jittery with shock and shame. Flambeau broke through the line of men and made for her.

She desperately tried to cover herself with the slip of African cloth she clutched in her hand. It was hopeless. Her nakedness floored Flambeau.

He faltered.

They looked at one another.

His small face worked to connect this ravaged woman with the one he once knew.

She saw his bewilderment. She held out her hand to him.

He just couldn't take it.

And then, very slowly, his mother looked away.

Eleanor could see she only had one shot before the rift was too wide for them ever to cross it. She shouted very loudly, 'Hey, Flambeau!'

She grabbed a blanket from the bench. 'Make it float.'

And she threw it to him.

To this day, neither of them could tell you what happened to that blanket as it flew through the air. Perhaps it was a heavy enough weave to build momentum as it flew? Maybe the touch of Flambeau's fingertips as it passed gave it the direction it needed? Whatever it was, Flambeau didn't even look back to see what was coming, he just lifted up his arms, focused his eyes like pinpricks and the blanket flew over his head. It hovered for a moment over his mother and then fell onto her shoulders.

# *Enough*

Eleanor hung onto the window of a very tall truck trying to talk sense to the driver inside it. He had just woken up and he wasn't expecting anyone to appear like a ghost at his window pleading for his help.

'Aye. There are three of us . . .' she said.

'Where are you off to then?' asked the driver.

'Not really fussed, just need to get to a bus stop, train station. We'll go wherever you're going.'

'I don't want trouble,' he said.

'No trouble. We're no trouble. Please.'

Flambeau and Bijou emerged from the truck wide-eyed with fright. He had the good sense to lead her into the protective shadow cast by a large truck.

Mother and son did not dare look at one another, but watched the tumble of men come out of the container in pursuit of them.

Far, far more ominously than that, a black hat loomed in the almost-dark of the truck door.

Flambeau would have known that silhouette anywhere.

He shouted out to Eleanor, 'Got to go. *Vite*. Got to go. HURRY!'

She could hear the seriousness in his voice and yet when she turned to open the truck door, the driver still slowly rolled his homemade cigarette and licked the paper. 'Come on, please! Yes or no, mate,' she implored him.

Manu stepped out of the shadows and made for Bijou. She saw him and screamed.

Neither Flambeau nor Eleanor would ever forget the fear in that cry.

The truck driver glanced up, 'Jesus! What was that?'

'Help us!' screamed Eleanor.

'Okay then. Bloody Hell. Get in.'

Eleanor fell into the passenger seat, and shouted, 'Run, Flambeau!'

Flambeau turned, but his mother did not follow.

Manu walked slowly towards her.

She saw him, but still she couldn't move.

Flambeau could see that Manu would knock her to the ground and drag her body across the stones. He could smell the defeat of it.

The boy gathered his forces and turned towards Manu, arms outstretched like a giant bird, mouth open, cawing.

The shock and surprise on Manu's face when he saw the roaring child coming towards him gave them just a fraction of time.

It was enough for Flambeau to swing his small body around, grab his mother's hand, and stumble across the muddy car park into the already moving cab.

# Black Road

'Bloody miserable night even for Scotland,' said the driver.

Not one of his passengers dared look at the other. They just rocked slightly to and fro with the movement of the vehicle.

The driver tried again. 'So where are you's headed?'

Nothing came back. Eleanor was beginning to feel sorry for him.

Then he said, 'Don't tell me . . . world's end . . . up here on the right.' He thought that would get a laugh out of them, but he didn't know who he was dealing with.

He shook his head and turned on the radio.

Eventually Flambeau and his mother fell asleep. Their two faces in repose were so alike and so peaceful that Eleanor couldn't take her eyes off them.

Flambeau's head leaned on the back of the front seat. Bijou's forward from the back seat. They were close enough to feel one another's breath.

It occurred to Eleanor right then that there was no more need of her.

You know.

She would have liked to think that she felt okay about it, but she didn't.

Her true love was dead. She could not go home to her ma for fear of rejection so profound she would never recover. And now she was going to be usurped in her only remaining reason for living.

The love and protection of Flambeau.

It was a measure of her fury that she found herself thinking. 'I never wanted to love Flambeau.' To her credit she didn't linger there long. It was over. That myth, at least, was over.


Eleanor gathered her forces as the hours of night rolled over her. In the breaking dawn, when the truck passed a remote bus stop she was ready.

She shouted, 'Hey Driver, pull over, will ya.'

Bijou and Flambeau woke with a start.

The truck stopped in the middle of the long black road. The door opened and nothing happened for a moment. Then Eleanor and her suitcase got out.

She stood by the side of the road.

Flambeau followed.

They turned to face one another.

His beautiful face looked up in that emerging-man kind of way that made her want to weep. She couldn't do it. She couldn't leave that face.

Then Flambeau, the child savant, took her hand and said, 'Where are you going to go, Eleanor the brave?'

She stepped right up close to him and she smelt him. She touched his cheek and whispered, 'You okay?'

'Okey-dokey,' he murmured.

And he nodded.

With that nod she was redeemed.

She said, 'Rome. Yeah. Maybe Rome.'

She looked around at the wind and space and flatness, and she thought. *I can do that.*

Flambeau pressed his face up against the back glass of the cabin and watched her as they drove away.

She watched him too.

Then he saw her turn and walk along the black road, her pink suitcase rolling along behind her.

She walked past the bus stop. She walked until she had wound her way to the top of the hill.

From there she could watch the truck barrel its way to the far distant end of the long black road.

# The Beach

The truck driver leant his back against the wheels of his parked truck and lit a cigarette. He closed his eyes.

The truck was parked on a rise that overlooked a beach and the sea beyond.

The small shape of Flambeau was making his way to the sea's edge. He pushed through wind and the soft sand to get there.

Bijou walked behind him, uncertain.

Then she stopped.

Her dark figure was very still in the whiteness.

Flambeau reached the line of breakers. He caught his breath, took in the openness of the sea. Just him and it.

He kicked off his shoes. Tucked one each into the top two pockets of his shirt.

The suck and pull of the waves onto the sand around his feet intoxicated him.

He turned away from it to look for his mother.

She was not there.

Not on the beach.

Not on the grasslands above the sand.

Not on the rocks.

He began to run.

He crested the dune and saw below him Bijou, with her legs outstretched in front of her, African style.

The smaller waves in the more protected cove broke over her legs. She didn't seem to notice. She was curled over into herself. She rocked and rocked.

And he watched her.

The African cloth wrapped half-heartedly around her abused body fluttered in the breeze.

A gust of wind stole it from her shoulders and sent it racing over the sand.

Flambeau shouted, 'Hey!'

But his mother did not look up.

He ran down onto the beach to retrieve it.


The cloth danced, teased, twitched across the sand. Flambeau pounced on it, missed, pounced again, got it.

He held it in his hands and turned to show her.


But his mother didn't look. She was walking into the waves. Aimlessly heading out to sea.

Flambeau watched her. Quizzical. Then he understood – she was never going to stop.

He shouted out, shrill and powerful. He shouted the only word on God's good earth that could stop her. He shouted, 'Mama!'

She turned. What did he say? Small waves hit her knees.

Flambeau moved towards her through the incoming tide.

She watched him approach.

He reached her.

The two of them looked at one another. She did not smile but watched him, wary.

She spoke very quietly. '*What did you say?*'

His answer did not come easily. '*I said . . . Mama.*'

She dipped her head down to survive the rush of feeling that the word evoked.

# *Rhumba*

The truck driver woke with a start. The end of his cigarette, burnt down to the tip, stung his lips with its heat.

He spat it out of his mouth and rubbed his hands over his face. He heard a sound. Singing. He looked up.

Flambeau and his mother, their shapes so black against the bleached white of the sand, were dancing.

At least that is what he thought they were doing, but when he looked again, they were merely walking.

Wait.

There it was again, just the slightest twist of the hip and a two-step, a flash.

Yes, they were dancing.


It was a tender, ironic Rhumba, slow and graceful on the white sands of the distant beach.

The truck driver stood up to see it better.

It was an exquisite sight, this dance. The pathos and cheek of it roughed up by the furious wind.

To say nothing of the impossibly long red cloth that rose up and danced mischief above them in the wild Scottish sky.

# *Acknowledgements*

Thanks to Shefali Malhoutra, old friend, who introduced this book to its editor and protector Shomit Mitter – who led it to its agent David Godwin – who gave it to its publisher Jon Riley – who saved its life, and mine. To my friend, Susanne Kapoor, who carried the flame. To Channel Four, who supported the initial research. To the BBC, who helped complete that process. To Margaret Matheson and Simon Channing-Williams, who – at different points – guided it along its way. To Anneke Von Woudenberg at Human Rights Watch, who, with the team in Goma, helped me learn the right way to say 'dusky turtle dove' in Kinyawranda and much, much more. And thanks to the music makers of the Congo, who have long kept hearts beating in troubled times.